Advanced Praise for

HIDDEN WOUNDS:
A SOLDIER'S BURDEN

"I am in awe of the work... Well done... this book will open conversations that need to happen for so many Soldiers. It is making an impact!"

— Lieutenant Colonel Tony P Burgess
U.S. Army, coauthor of *Taking the Guidon*

"A compelling story of family and war, of what tears people apart and what brings them together. This book touched my heart. It opens the way for a better understanding of war's lasting wounds, especially PTSD."

— Toni Bernhard, author of *How to Be Sick*,
winner of the 2011 Gold Nautilus Book
Award in Self-Help/Psychology

"A winner... thoroughly enjoyable reading"

— Colonel (Ret) Mike Valdez
Oregon National Guard, Vietnam veteran

HIDDEN WOUNDS

A Soldier's Burden

NATE BROOKSHIRE
& MARIUS TECOANTA

Network 3000 Publishing

© 2012 by Nate Brookshire and Marius Tecoanta

Requests for permission to make copies of any part of the work should be submitted online to meta@ix.netcom.com or mailed to the following address: Permissions Dept., Network 3000 Publishing, 16526 W. 78th St. #138, Eden Prairie, MN 55346

www.network3000publishing.com

Library of Congress Cataloging-in-Publication Data has been applied for.

ISBN 978-1-934266-22-9

Printed in the United States of America

Cover Design by Elle Phillips & Chris DeLoach
Book Design by Elle Phillips

Please direct foreign rights inquiries to: meta@ix.netcom.com

Dedicated to Military Spouses;
heroes without medals.

Acknowledgements

Nate Brookshire and Marius Tecoanta want to sincerely thank everyone involved in conveying the message of *Hidden Wounds: A Soldier's Burden*.

To Melanie Brookshire and Rodica Tecoanta for their patience, assistance and love.

To Team Brookshire, Dr. Kevin Hogan, Katie Hogan, Helena Kaufman, Elle Phillips, James Burns, Chris De Loach and Anna Bigham for making this book possible.

To Col (Ret.) Mike Valdez, Col (Ret.) Richard Swengros, LTC (Ret.) Gordon Cucullu, LTC Tony Burgess, Carl Prine, SGM (Ret.) Mark Hlasnicek, Dr. Nancy Brown, Dr. Katherine Carroll, Dr. Toni Bernhard for their advice and support.

To Gary Sinise, Roger Sicely, Aaron Arp, Mark McConnaughhay, Terry Snow, Phillip Cockrell, Phillip Lenz, William Coulter, Chad Ashe, Jeff Krohn, Buzz Krohn, Christina Olds, Ed Roth, Phil Nerges, Steve Diaz, Dan Ramsey, Brad O'Brien, Bruce Aho, Brian Ferguson, Ben Feicht, Chris Vincent, Tammy Duckworth, Mike Mehling, Gordon Key, Amber Gloria, April Braswell, Helmut Foertsch, Chris Alexander, Rafael Taft, Charles Baker, Brett Brandon, Sheila Van Dyke, Eddie McDevitt, Ed Hamlin, Darrell Sides, Chris Wickman, Noel & Cary Nelson, Michael Schmidt, Jay Carter, Bill Carter, Huw Thomas, Donald Howell, Dale Bell, Laurie Bell, Scott Bell, Naomi Bettencourt, Julie Broad, Alexander Christiani, Deborah Cole, Cindy Dachuk, Terry Frazier,

Shannon Fullmer, Alam Ghafoor, Menaz Ghafoor, David Graska, Josh Gretz, Christian Haller, Peter Helton, Donald Hendon, Larry Hines, Lyle Johnson, Diane LaMadrid, Bill Lampe, Diane Lampe, Brian Latta, Bryan Lenihan, Gary May, Roberto Monaco, Rob Northrup, Victoria Olson, Ken Owens, Eva Palmer, Jeff Paro, Andrew Records, Art Remnet, Tim Guffey, Jessica Martin and Ray Taeger for their contribution, encouragement and suggestions.

Special thanks to our Editor for being a coach, mentor and above all else, friend.

Any errors are the sole responsibility of the authors.

Foreword

War does for human emotions what a laser does for light particles: gathers and intensifies them to the point that they can make us blind. Throughout *Hidden Wounds: A Soldier's Burden* we see how the experiences of war – even over decades – can render one unable to perceive behavior that is obvious to others.

A tired cliché says that "time heals all wounds." But for those who have endured the trauma, the seemingly endless passage of time affords one only the dubious opportunity to dwell, relive, question, and regret. Their experience becomes an endless-loop movie that always plays in the forefront of their minds.

A cruel penchant of the human mind is its ability to sow doubt, second-guess, and ultimately despair. While we may acknowledge at the conscious, intellectual level that split-second decisions made in combat cannot bear detailed analysis, our vicious subconscious – that "little voice in our heads" – is always there to undermine our best intentions. Perhaps one of the most oft-repeated themes one hears in talking to those who have endured extreme stress is the frustratingly unanswerable question: What could I have done differently?

Hidden Wounds adroitly explores the ramifications of what can happen to an otherwise outstanding American Soldier when plagued to the point of instability over decades by that terrible voice. All it took in this case was a single, isolated but poignant incident to alter the life of a man and his family. Too often that is the case with returning combat veterans.

Most tragically, much of his anguish was self-inflicted. By his inability to come to terms with the reality of the situation, and by feeding his angst with a secret, constant reminder of that day, his guilt morphed from self-criticism into a self-destructive quest.

The story told in *Hidden Wounds* is not allegorical: these things happen on a daily basis to American servicemen and women. Haunted by nightmares, struggling to cope with routine civilian activities, troubled by memories that they vainly attempt to alter or erase, they often stumble through their lives, going through the motions but failing to fit back into the comfort zone they enjoyed prior to combat. To some degree or another almost every returning combat veteran – Soldier or civilian contractor – shares that experience.

In *Hidden Wounds*, we see a Soldier who was haunted by his past but still able outwardly to function. Aside from those closest to him, few others, including his pastor, had an inkling that something deeply troubling possessed his waking thoughts.

By contrast, not all combat veterans are able to maintain even a façade of normality. Others, like the main character, focus inward, and only family and close friends at most feel the effects. Anger, family conflicts, and employment issues trouble today's veterans. Substance abuse – in this story alcohol – is all too common a palliative. Predominantly, they are conflicted by an inability to deprogram themselves from a life on edge, with mortal danger or terrible wounding often seconds away, into what they see as a placid, slow-paced, relatively uneventful civilian society.

Over the past decades, we've called it many things:

shell shock, battle fatigue, the thousand-yard stare, and post-traumatic stress disorder. It was once considered a sign of weakness, of cowardice; and the stigma persists despite sincere efforts to mitigate it. Regardless of the label, the issue needs to be addressed, even in – perhaps especially in – those who pretend that they are immune.

After months of living with a weapon always at hand, many feel naked, vulnerable, and helpless. Loud, abrupt sounds send their heartbeats racing, all senses on alert. Everyday problems – entirely routine for a civilian population such as finances, children, relationships, and social events – appear trivial at best, and distracting at worst.

Some of the more seriously affected – an unacceptably high percentage – decide that death is preferable to an inability to cope with life. Suicide rates as a consequence are tragically off the charts with returning Soldiers and combat zone civilians – the latter shamefully underreported.

While conventional assistance is available in the form of psychological counseling, some Soldiers reject it as useless, and for many it is. Few professionals have more than theoretical knowledge of battlefield realities and are mired deep in the academic swamps of early 20th century mental health theoreticians. In a flawed, but well-meaning effort to help, their training and temperament guides psychiatrists and counselors to prescribe mood-altering drugs, primarily used to treat depression. "I'm not depressed," several Soldiers have said. "It's what I went through downrange."

Many of the medications come with deleterious side effects. "I was taking more than ten prescriptions and the drugs made me impotent," one senior non-commissioned officer said. "And now my wife thinks I'm having an affair." More than one Soldier has died merely by following medical orders and ingesting a lethal cocktail of mixed antidepressants and stimulants.

We send young people away – to camp, college, first

job, or boarding school – and marvel at the changes when they return home. Yet inexplicably we persist in pretending that Soldiers returning from the cauldron of war will magically re-adjust and pick up where they left off without missing a beat. In a phrase, that dog won't hunt.

There are as many ways for Soldiers to recalibrate their lives as there are Soldiers. Each usually finds a solution that works best or somehow forces the round peg into the square hole to the point of being able to function. So why do we assume that one solution fits all? Perhaps it is in the nature of a bureaucracy to attempt to standardize and rationalize people in the same manner as is done with equipment. Certainly it is easier, requires less thought, and shows better on a Power Point presentation that way. However, America is smart, innovative, and creative. We can do a better job.

Make no mistake: this is not a job for the military alone, or even the massive bureaucracy of government, although those institutions have key roles and responsibilities. This task devolves on us, the 99% of the American population who are quite content to allow the dedicated 1% to perform our heavy lifting in foreign conflicts while we enjoy life here. These are America's sons and daughters and we have a citizen's responsibility to help them.

Thankfully, America is seeing a rise in organizations dedicated to assisting combat Soldiers while treating them as responsible, growing adults. While officialdom is slow to catch on to the trend, already individuals and groups provide Soldiers with a productive work environment among their peers and the opportunity to do something mentally and physically challenging while keeping their dignity intact.

In Iraq and Afghanistan, I too frequently heard what has become a fairly consistent Soldier's refrain: "America's not at war," they say. "We're at war. America's at the mall."

It is our shame that we have allowed the situation to sink this deep. We need to take individual action to get involved with these Soldiers. If we are not going to pick up a weapon and stand a watch, then the least we can do is be tangibly grateful – by actions, not words – for those who make the sacrifice.

— LTC (Ret.) Gordon Cucullu

Gordon Cucullu, together with his wife Chris Fontana, is co-founder of the Valhalla Project, designed to assist post-9/11 combat Soldiers. Their most recent book is *Warrior Police: Rolling with America's Military Police in the World's Trouble Spots*, due for release in September 2011. Learn more about Valhalla at www.valhalla-project.com.

PROLOGUE

The metal detector's buzz startled John. His frown and evident displeasure cued the female deputy to use her most polite smile.

"Do you have anything else in your pockets, sir?"

"Not a damn thing!" John snarled, holding his beltless pants with his hands. The old man's frustration grew as she scanned him with her wand. The wand beeped around John's legs.

"Do you have a metal plate, sir?"

"Oh… yes!" He had forgotten about the orthopedic hardware. "I have some plates, pins, screws and whatever else the doctor used to fix my broken ankle."

He collected his wallet and his belt.

"Are we done here?"

"Please proceed through the glass double doors, sir. Make sure you have the bail receipt and two photo IDs."

John turned to Margarie. He tried to sound supportive, "Let's get Mike."

***

The heavy metal doors swung open.

"Get up! Looks like you are out of here."

Mike stood up. He knew this particular deputy all too well.

"Mean son-of-a-bitch… I would be upset too if I

was sweating like that all the time," Mike thought. Mike couldn't stand the look on the guard's face. He had seen the look too many times from his teachers, pastor, boy scout leaders and especially his own father... to him it was the look of disappointed disgust - and he could not escape it.

Mike caught a glimpse of his dad standing just past the glass doors. His stomach churned and he braced himself for the lecture. He knew it by heart and in some strange way it was familiar. At least he would get his dad's full attention - even if it was only for a few short minutes.

He waited patiently to get back his personal effects and took a deep breath before going out to greet his parents. This was not going to be a pleasant reunion. His dad just turned and headed for the door.

As they walked to the car in silence, he could see the distance between his mom and dad. Trailing behind, he thought for a moment that he might just get left in the parking lot. Mike touched his mom's shoulder, "They don't have anything. All they found was an empty syringe. It will never hold up in court and I will sue them for this drama." John quickly closed the distance between them and grabbed Mike's arm, digging in his fingers, "Get in the car! Save your lies for your lawyer."

It was just a few minutes from the jail to Mike's apartment. The streets were empty and Mike could feel the car speeding up. Margarie could not hold back anymore and started crying quietly.

"Oh, c'mon Mom... I'm telling you, the cops didn't have any reason to arrest me this time. I'm clean now."

John intervened:

"When was the last time you talked with your brother, Mike?"

"Which one, J.J. or Brant?"

"Stop being a smartass! You know I am talking about

John Junior. You do owe him money, don't you?"

"Yeah, Dad… but I have this gig now and after that I am planning to get that seasonal job at the lake. I'll pay him, you know I will."

"No, I don't. I know you always have a plan to pay him, but you never do…"

The car stopped in front of an aging apartment complex. Paint was peeling on every surface and the wooden stairs appeared to be near collapse. Mike was glad to jump out.

"Thanks, Mom, Dad. I'll talk to you soon. By the way, there is no food in the fridge right now. Can you help me out until I cash my unemployment check?"

"NO!" boomed John.

"Well, no big deal. Thanks again, Dad."

"Mike…"

"Yes, Mom?"

"You have food in your fridge, and we took care of your phone bill."

Mike caught his mom's eyes. She had always been there for him. If only he could be what she saw.

"Thanks again, Mom. Love you!"

Mike's words were cut short as the old station wagon lurched forward, turned onto the main road and was gone.

***

Margarie stood in the walk-in closet gently touching John's barely worn dress uniform. The uniform had twenty ribbons on it and included a Bronze Star. She thumbed the small V on the ribbon, knowing it meant nothing to her husband. John would just add ribbons as they were awarded. Every five years, while on active duty, he got the required photos, but he would never wear it in public, no matter what the occasion. John had always chosen his black suit over his dress uniform. She knew the reason for this choice… and it was buried somewhere in Germany. She looked over her shoulder and saw him sleeping. If only Mike would keep his promises… and John could let go of the past.

Margarie still felt a pang of guilt about the way they met. She could only imagine John's anger if he found out that she had kept secrets from him. Too often, she had watched John getting numb using whiskey to self-medicate. She knew that Mike was not the cause. John was a good man; however, his world was grey. He was stuck in the past, trying to make right something he couldn't. Margarie, with all the love she had to give, could not restore his soul. She knew that John craved a forgiveness that had already been given… the only problem was… he did not know it yet.

She thought of her recent visit to the cardiologist - time was not on her side. She had chosen not to give the details to John, and spent her energy preparing everything for him just in case. She wanted their last days together to be peaceful, and not filled with anger and rage at something they could not control. Margarie didn't know if it was right - but the one thing she did know was that John would make everyone's life a living hell trying to save her.

ONE LAST JOURNEY

"The burden of dead faces. Out of sight
And out of love, beyond the reach of hands,
Changed in the changing of the dark and light,
They walk and weep about the barren lands..."

A. C. SWINBURNE

John Dougall shuffled to the window, the air conditioning and the disinfectant smell was causing him to panic. He mustered all the strength left in his ailing body and raised the heavy sliding panel. Cool, spring air rushed in. It felt like life itself. Energized, John took a deep breath and whispered: "O Lord; forgive me the sins of my youth."

He had come from a long line of hardened men forged by tough times. His father had fought in France in 1918 and his grandfather had seen service in the Spanish-American War. Obsessed from an early age with knowing his family roots, John had discovered the Dougalls, with two Ls, had arrived in America in 1670.

The first John Dougall, an indentured servant, had spent seven years working off his passage from Scotland. During this time he had raised two sons, Mannering and James. Their descendants had turned west to settle their ever growing families. Mannering's branch had ventured to Kentucky. John's roots in Tennessee dated back to James taking another path.

And so it went in John's daily practice of recollecting the family lineage he knew so well. This mind game helped him pass the time in the Veterans Administration nursing home. Today, for some reason, he could not remember the link between his great-grandfather and Mannering's side of the clan. Considering that he hadn't had a visitor in weeks, this mental exercise seemed to bring both comfort and anxiety. Comfort because his memory was still there for the most part, and anxiety because his great- grandchildren would ultimately not know much about the Dougall history, unless he had a chance to pass on some of that history himself. His most urgent need in the world had become telling his very own story.

Now at the age of eighty-four, life was going to grant him that chance. If he missed the opportunity – the truth would die with him. His youngest son, Brant, was coming for him.

Together, they would return to Germany. He would hold a granddaughter he had never met and walk the grounds of former battles. Maybe this trip would bring the closure he needed to lift the burden on his soul; the one that lingered.

Getting ready for the journey had taken John days of mental preparation and only one hour of actual packing. When the nurse came by to check his blood pressure for the last time before his departure, John wanted to let someone know that he was not coming back.

"I have traveled a lot in my life and have never bought a ticket. Uncle Sam paid for all my trips. Now, I am ready to spend my way out of here."

The nurse did not respond. John noticed the earphones and chuckled softly.

"You can't hear me, can you?"

The nurse caught his grin and pulled one of the earphones out.

"Did you say something, Mr. Dougall?"

"Talking to myself... nothing important... "

John had been in the VA nursing home for the past three years. After his wife, Margarie, passed away, he was unable to fully care for himself. They had three sons. John Jr., the oldest, was a retired Marine living with his family in Beaufort, South Carolina. Brant, the youngest, was an Army non-commissioned officer, stationed in Germany, getting ready for his own path to retirement. Mike, the middle son, was still living in Columbia, South Carolina where the Dougalls had made their home when John retired from the Army. Always the "black sheep," Mike had spent most of his adult life in and out of jail, so John could not count on his support now. Considering the circumstances, the VA nursing home was his only option. The first sign that John could not depend on his sons was at Margarie's funeral. Margarie had died suddenly of a heart attack. As a dedicated organizer, she had left behind a detailed list of how she wanted things to be.

The expectation of her sons returning home to support each other and to help their father was not met. So, as John stood by her grave with the small group from their church, he realized that he would need to seek out the help of the VA. His inability to take care of himself and need for care landed him in the nursing home; arriving with only a duffel bag, a few books and his signature retiree hat noting his service in WWII, Korea and Vietnam. Being drafted at the age of eighteen allowed him this claim to fame that few had on their record.

In those three years, he had received visitors from the church, a few well-meaning veterans and one visit each from his older sons. Mike was the first to come by to see him. The purpose of his visit was simply to find out what he would receive from the estate of his mother; needless to say, it did not go well and Mike left spewing expletives about how he deserved more. John Jr. came to announce his third marriage. The visit was brief and filled with promises of staying in touch. Both knew those were likely just empty words.

John Dougall longed to also see his youngest son. When Brant called unexpectedly to announce his upcoming arrival, the old man was elated.

***

Brant looked over at Tanja, his pregnant wife. They had just spent a three-day weekend with some of her family in the Bavarian Forest. She was absolutely radiant and he couldn't imagine what life would be like without her. Occasionally, he felt unconditional happiness wash over him. Those moments were rare.

After returning from Iraq, it seemed his emotions were frozen, neither high nor low, just a steady numbness. His drinking was getting more excessive just to get even a weak buzz. Tanja did notice that he had gone from his usual couple of beers a night to a six-pack plus a couple of shots of whiskey. The weekend in the Bavarian Forest had been a much needed getaway forced by Tanja. Brant did his part. He limited his alcohol intake except on Saturday night when one of Tanja's local German friends challenged him shot for shot on a bottle of whiskey; her friend was still in bed sleeping it off when they left Sunday evening.

Brant's cell phone rang and he could see "Wild Bill" on the screen. His battle buddy, Bill Humphrey, was calling and he knew he should answer. They had made dinner plans with him before heading out to the woods and now they were running late to meet him.

"Brant, brother... I can't make it to dinner tonight with you. This job is really ruining my social life."

Brant could tell that something major had happened from Bill's tone.

"Wild Bill, what you got going on? You counting widgets again? I told you that being an operations sergeant sucks, almost as bad as being at Battalion."

"No, man. We just had a soldier blow his brains out and the First Sergeant wants me to make sure everything is taken care of. The boss is freaking out, thinking this is going to stain her career. It's just crazy, man. She didn't even blink about the soldier. She just started asking all these crazy questions and it was pretty clear who she is concerned about... herself."

"I am sorry to hear that, brother... What's the soldier's name?"

"Specialist Kowalski."

Brant could not respond. He felt all the air escape his lungs.

"Ah, man, I'm sorry. I just realized he was one of your guys from your old platoon. I am just about as bad as the freaking Captain. Sorry, I'll keep you posted on what's going on... sorry again for being an ass, just a lot going on right now."

"Brant, what is wrong? Can you tell me? Please... keep your eyes on the road. You are scaring me with your driving; you know that you shouldn't be on the phone and driving at the same time." Tanja's hands instinctively moved to her belly.

Brant turned to Tanja and simply stated:

"Kowalski is dead."

They rode the rest of the way in silence. Once home, Brant immediately got into his uniform and went to see Bill. As Brant walked into the office, he saw the battalion operations Sergeant Major standing at Bill's desk.

"Sergeant Dougall, what are you doing here?"

"Sergeant Major, Specialist Kowalski was one of my soldiers during the last rotation - I just want to see what I can do. That platoon's already taken a lot of hits; most of them are just now coming to terms with the loss of their buddies from the first Iraq rotation."

Bill finished briefing the Sergeant Major on the time-line, his interaction with Mortuary Affairs, and the details of the memorial service.

"Sergeant Major, the only thing we haven't closed the loop on is the military escort."

Sergeant Major turned to Brant. It was unspoken yet understood... Brant would take his soldier home.

***

Brant had not planned to return to the United States before his own upcoming deployment back to Iraq. Specialist George Kowalski's suicide changed that. Kowalski had been Brant's gunner in their last rotation to Iraq. He was a strong-willed Chicagoan who wanted to engage the enemy at every chance and grumble at every opportunity. As a freshly-promoted platoon sergeant, Sergeant First Class Brant Dougall found his integration into a seasoned platoon bumpy at best. It took time to earn the trust of the squad leaders, some of them almost as experienced as he was. The good part was that the Lieutenant trusted him and let Brant run the show.

Kowalski, however, was one of the few that needed extra attention and patience. He had a habit of listening intently to any briefing and then asking questions, pointing out meaningless errors or minor inconsistencies, driving his superiors crazy. There was always a sense that Kowalski was seeking attention through rebellion, and in many of these moments Brant was reminded of his older brother Mike. Living with Mike's shenanigans over the years had made Brant indifferent to someone lashing out at authority. When Kowalski saw that he was not getting any reaction from his new platoon sergeant, he gradually morphed into one of Brant's best soldiers. After defusing and then gaining the trust of the skeptical Specialist, Sergeant Dougall found he had a loyal and efficient gunner to protect him in Iraq.

***

At 0400 Brant arrived at the funeral home and met with Wild Bill. They walked into the building and found a guy from the funeral home's staff sleeping in a row of chairs by the coffin. The man sprung up and greeted them in German...

"*Guten Morgen.*"

"*Guten Morgen, sprechen Sie* English?"

"Yes, I do."...The man went straight to the coffin and opened it.

The shock of seeing Specialist Kowalski in his uniform with his hands folded together took Brant aback. His immediate reaction was to reach out and touch Kowalski's hand.

"It is OK. Go ahead and touch him. They did a really good job on him considering."

Brant looked at the man in disbelief; the German had not realized that they knew the soldier personally. "He was a great soldier and a fine man," said Brant looking straight at the German.

The man looked embarrassed and said that he would get the vehicle ready for the trip to the airport. About that time an older gentleman joined them.

"Good morning. I'm Rob Wesson from Mortuary Affairs. I am here to go with you to the airport and make sure that you understand your duties as a military escort."

Brant and Wesson inspected Kowalski's uniform and placed the American flag over the coffin. Brant remembered reading an article written by a Marine Lieutenant Colonel about his experience escorting a fallen Marine home. Little did he know that he would be called to the same duty and how much that article would prepare him for this emotional journey.

Wesson drove and talked Brant through the procedures: the requirement to inspect the remains every time there was a stop in the movement of the casket and to render honors. Brant's job would not be complete until he signed over the remains to the funeral director in Columbia, South Carolina. The Casualty Assistance Officer would coordinate with the family to meet Brant, if they chose to do so. The Commander, First Sergeant and several of the platoon members had been flown back from Germany to attend the funeral. Another officer from the unit had arranged for most of Specialist Kowalski's personal effects to be brought back.

Mr. Wesson talked about his time on active duty in Mortuary Affairs. He had been at Fort Campbell during the Gander crash that claimed the lives of two hundred and forty-eight soldiers and eight crewmen. The details of what Wesson experienced during the aftermath of that tragedy made Brant very uncomfortable. He almost regretted his decision to volunteer for military escort duty.

When they arrived at the airport, the process became very logistical. Looking at the white shipping box, he could not process that his soldier was laying there. Wesson looked at him and simply said:

"This is a zero-defect job. Honor your soldier and get him home to his family. Don't deviate from what I have told you. This is a time-honored tradition that ensures our soldiers get a proper burial. Your actions will be remembered by the family, and by those who see you conducting the escort. Get it right."

Brant could see the tears in Wesson's eyes. He knew that this was more than a job to him. He promised Wesson that he would fulfill his duty.

***

Until Brant's short phone call, John had lived in a dark, self-imposed exile. His daily thoughts had become a prison and his old body was his solitary confinement. He had to endure to get to the end of his sentence.

He did not complain once. Whining never helped,

and what was there to complain about? He felt he deserved everything.

The old soldier understood that Brant's coming home had everything to do with another tragedy. Personally, this reunion was the highlight of the last three years. Shrugging off a nagging tinge of selfishness, John allowed himself to feel almost happy.

"The ever-generous Brant," thought John. "Now it's up to me. This is my chance… my last chance. Then, when the Journal is returned and my sins are there for everyone to see, I will face my judgment… and I'll finally join Margarie."

While waiting for Brant to pick him up, the nurse came by and asked if it was alright for Pastor Thomas to visit. John nodded. He felt relieved that at least someone in town knew the details of his upcoming adventure. What they didn't know was that he did not plan to return.

"Hi, John. So what's going on with the luggage?"

"Well, Pastor, they say you can't take it with you – I am going to try and prove them wrong." John said this with a smirk, all the while knowing that it wouldn't take much to stir the pastor into a full blown sermon on "going home."

"John, I can see it in your face that you are baiting me… but I am not biting today. I am really concerned with what is going on with you – not only your mental health, but your spiritual health. I know Margarie's passing pushed you into isolation and the situation with Mike isn't helping. I heard Brant is coming to take you back to Germany. How are you feeling about that?"

John looked at the pastor and felt a tinge of anger. He could see the pastor's thought process. Margarie and John had been in the church for over forty years, and it seemed that there wasn't a thing about them that the pastor did not know. John wanted to shout: "You do not know anything about me and what I did; you have no idea who I am!"

Instead, he said quietly:

"I have a grandchild I have never met, sons I don't really know and a dead wife whose passing has left me incapable of taking care of myself. I say that with all the love in the world for her, but I depended so much on her that I am basically at a loss. I am alone and now I have a chance to change that... for a while."

Brant stepped into the room, still in full dress uniform having just returned from the cemetery. His face showed how absolutely drained he was from all the travel and the emotion of bringing his dead soldier home. Looking at Brant in his uniform, John was thankful that Margarie had decided to have another child. John's mind moved quickly to Mike and felt guilt at not having the same pride, and for that matter, love for his middle son. He wondered how they could be so different. He questioned if his anger towards Mike came from the pain his rebel son caused Margarie, or from Mike being a reflection of John's own faults as a man and a father.

"Dad, ready to go?" Brant said, glancing at Pastor Thomas.

"Brant, you remember the pastor – he's been one of the only steady visitors I get here."

"Brant, I am sorry to hear about your soldier – these are difficult times, and these wars just seem to never end." Pastor Thomas slowly touched Brant's shoulder with a look of compassion.

Brant bristled at the pastor's touch.

"Who exactly are you sorry for? This soldier put a gun to his head and blew his brains out, and I just spent the last couple of hours with his family – not sure I would chalk it up to 'difficult times' and wondering about a timeline on when this war will end. He had a family. He had friends who cared for him, and he still chose to take himself out because his conscience would not let him rest at having taken a life."

The pastor did not react. He quietly offered:

"Brant, I am truly sorry, and I hope you can forgive yourself and your soldier someday. If it is any comfort – look at this loss as yet another casualty of this war."

The statement washed over Brant. Under John's curious stare, Brant regained composure. Exhaling deeply, he responded in a low, deferential tone:

"Pastor, thanks. I am sorry for talking to you that way. I was raised better."

Father and son both waited patiently for the pastor to end his visit and say goodbye. When Brant cleared his throat, he looked at his father for his disapproval. Secretly, John enjoyed how his Brant made the pastor shorten his visit. With a chuckle he let him off the hook.

"Well, Son, you are not the smoothest of the bunch are you? Forget Thomas… I've gotten tired of that preacher too. You need a soldier to understand a soldier."

THE JOURNAL

Every man is guilty of all the good he did not do.

VOLTAIRE

It had been more than forty years since John had flown overseas. The last time was on his return from Southeast Asia, serving as one of the advisors for the Military Assistance Command Vietnam (MACV). On that flight he already knew that he would soon retire, and then he'd stay put for as long as he could possibly manage. His tumultuous career and those demons from his past took a heavy toll on his family. Often, John questioned his own mental sanity. He coped with everything by erecting walls between himself and others. His aloofness lead some to believe he was eccentric, or at the very least, quirky.

"I've let this fester for too long." The thoughts of self-loathing came fast and without warning. This time, John did not fight it with countless justifications. The determination to end the pain once and for all gave him a sense of urgency. The self-worth he chased in the rugged hills of Korea and in the swamps of Vietnam was futile. "It is time," John mumbled to himself.

"Dad, you're packing pretty light. Is that going to be enough for a month?" Brant's question snapped him out of his reverie. Without waiting for an answer Brant added,

"Let me change and we'll head to the airport."

John looked at his suitcase and realized that it held all that he had left in the world. Everything in the house had been sold or given to charity, except three changes of clothes, his favorite shoes, his worn-out hat and his most cherished possession; the Journal.

✳✳✳

Brant feared that his dad had already resigned himself to not coming back to the VA. He knew John was being consumed by something in his past, something related to the leather bound notebook he'd seen his father hold onto since the war.

Growing up, Brant had always wondered where the notebook had come from. He often found his dad passed out in his favorite chair, holding it, guarding it, as if with his life. The black, leather-bound Journal, held so closely, was rarely opened, and never discussed. Over the years, he had seen it on occasions when his father would bring it out after a few drinks. During these rare times, John Dougall would sit in his chair, stare into the distance and thumb the leather strap that kept the Journal closed and secure.

Those periods of palpable glumness threw the whole family into a tailspin. Brant often pondered if Mike's rebellious attitude sprung from John's aloofness. Watching their father self-medicate over the years was something that marked everyone. John never hid his alcohol intake, but he didn't make it readily known, either. He always waited for the night time and never got quite drunk. He seemed to drink just enough to calm himself. He always got that same faraway look.

* * *

The airport was pretty quiet, and they were three hours early for their flight to Atlanta, after which they'd catch a connection to Germany.

Typical military preparation, thought John.

He remembered how he had preferred to do backwards planning all his life. Brant picked up the habit. He always put in a little extra cushion of time when it came to traveling. John didn't mind the extra wait time at all, until he looked up and saw Mike running down the terminal's hall towards them.

"Brant, what the hell is Mike doing here?"

"Dad, I'm sorry. He wanted to see you before you left, and I knew that you wouldn't have agreed to see him at the hospital. It's better to be in a public place anyway, so there won't be a scene."

John jumped up from his seat as Mike reached them; it was amazing how the military posture came back so quickly. Gasping for air, Mike began...

"Dad, I know you don't want to see me... I just want to say goodbye and that... I am sorry."

John looked at Mike. The rage inside him welled up. He thought about all the times Margarie cried over Mike's reckless antics over the years.

"What the hell are you doing, Mike? You're a forty-five-year-old man. Why are you running here like a teenager wanting forgiveness now?"

"Dad, I am sorry for what I did to you and Mom," said Mike trembling. "I can't explain why I am what I am, but I am doing the best I can with what I've got. I can't even say that I'm going to change. I just wanted to let you know that I do recognize the pain I've caused you, and I want to know if you can find it in yourself to say goodbye without looking at me with disgust and hate."

John sat down, looked at Brant, and then back at Mike. It seemed that nothing ever went right with Mike. Having sons so far apart in age brought major challenges and put a lot of pressure on Margarie. His mind ached when he remembered his wife. She had been his family's glue.

He had met Margarie in 1958 while stationed in Bamberg, Germany. They married right before John left to return to the states on his way to Fort Campbell. The way they met was always just told as a simple statement of fact to the boys with no details. John was in his early thirties and

Margarie had just turned twenty.

Margarie arrived at Fort Campbell, Kentucky, a newlywed, at the young age of twenty-one, still trying to figure out not only the Army lingo, but also the American culture. She had been on an exchange program from Wales when their paths crossed. John was more than twelve years her senior but his broken German had amused her when they first met at the Dance Hall in the Weyermann Malt Factory. He was surprised to discover that she was British. They talked for hours and John was soon captivated with her.

Margarie had urged him to retire because she thought additional deployments would put Mike through the same turmoil that John Jr. experienced during John's tours to Vietnam. It had taken years to get little John to stop clinging to his father every time he left the house. She did not want to go through the same with Mike.

John retired with the intention of spending as much time at home as he could. He yearned to make up for the time he felt he had lost as a husband and father. His career inspired John Jr. to join the Marines, and Brant, to join the Army. John knew that he pushed his sons hard, sometimes too hard. He felt compelled to teach them how to make the right choices, no matter the consequences.

With Mike, the "tough love" approach had somehow backfired. Now, John was staring at a middle-aged man who was still making life decisions like a sixteen-year-old. John didn't hate Mike, and he wasn't disgusted, just angry.

"Mike, I am angry that we weren't good enough parents to protect you from yourself. I'm so sorry that you see hate and disgust in my eyes. If it is there, it is a reflection of what is inside of me. I only wish we had done things differently. We should have spent more time helping you discover who you are versus trying to make you what we thought you should be.

Your mother dealt with the harsh realities of separation

while I was off 'gallivanting' around the world. It was not fair to our family, but it was what we saw as our duty. We know it was fulfilled at a cost. I am just now, at the end of my life, realizing how high that price truly was. I forgive you. Now, can you forgive me? Don't change for me. Change for yourself."

* * *

Mike stood. He hugged John silently, nodded to Brant and left the airport. He felt like he was walking on air. Mike felt that he had finally received forgiveness from his father, the man he had spent so many years fighting. He did not know why he felt so betrayed by his parents. On the surface, they were always there for him... but he needed more.

John Jr. was all boy and so was his younger brother, Brant. In contrast, Mike did not like camping, boy scouts, sports, or anything to do with conformity. He preferred listening to music in his room and being alone. This drove John and Margarie to the edge, considering their level of participation in the church and the community.

Most evenings were marked by John lecturing Mike on how he had embarrassed the family. It seemed to be a cycle he could not break. Mike became the resident expert on pushing the right buttons to get his father into drill sergeant mode.

As Mike got into his car, a barely street-legal piece of junk with expired tags, the euphoric feeling suddenly stopped. The prize of forgiveness soon left him feeling very stupid. He had wasted his youth in a state of continuous rebellion against his parents; when in fact, they had tried all along to show him their unconditional love and support. All he could do was drive to his mother's grave side and sit, wondering where he would be now if he had not taken the path he was on, and what, if anything, he could do to change direction.

"Are people entitled to a second chance? ...Or a fiftieth, in my case?" Mike breathed deeply and tried to draw strength from remembering his favorite Bible parable, the Prodigal Son.

***

John watched Mike walk away, knowing it would be the last time that they would meet. He was okay with it. He felt content sitting in the Atlanta airport with his youngest son. They watched uniformed soldiers make their way to connecting flights; some just returning from war and some finally heading home for good. He remembered crossing the Atlantic the first time; a series of trains, ships, buses and even a horse-drawn cart got him to his destination in southern England to join his unit. He didn't know it at the time, but in less than six months he would be a part of the D-Day invasion.

"Private Dougall, welcome to the 3rd Army!" yelled First Sergeant Young. "Glad you could join us before the war is over. By the size of you, it looks like you are going to serve as a replacement in the Military Police platoon attached to the headquarters."

John's mind was a blur. He was not at all sure about what was going on around him. Now he was being told he was going to be assigned to MP duties? One thing that had served him well was to stand at a rigid position of attention, or parade rest, when told to do so and sound off with "Yes" followed by whatever rank was in front of him. So far in his career this tactic had worked really well... why chance it and do something different.

"Yes, First Sergeant!" John sounded off at the top of his

lungs.

"Yes to what? I didn't ask you a damn question, Private. Hopefully, I am not making a mistake sending you to the Palace Guard platoon. You look the part, but those officers will eat you alive if you're stupid. I'll chalk it up to nerves and send you there anyway. Go see Staff Sergeant McGee two tents down on your left and get settled in. Dismissed."

John hesitated, saluted, and ran out of the tent. First Sergeant Young shook his head, and mumbled,

"Confirmed stupid... saluting a First Sergeant. I should have sent him to the mess section to scrub pans."

* * *

Brant and John made their way to the check-in counter at the airline. Brant was still on official orders from his military escort duties.

"Would you like an upgrade?"

Brant looked at the young woman behind the counter. She was smiling.

"Do you have two seats together? I'm traveling with my father."

"Of course," she replied.

Brant had refused the First Class seat he was offered on his flight in from Germany. He was surprised to find out the airline's personnel and fellow passengers knew about his duty to escort the remains of a soldier home. What he didn't know was that the Captain had made an announcement to the passengers about his solemn duty while he was on the tarmac rendering honors. Now, boarding the plane with his father, he felt at ease. He thought that this trip would be a good opportunity to break down the walls between him and his old man. He knew it might be his last opportunity.

The flight attendant stopped at their seats and leaned

over so close to Brant that he could see her cleavage and smell her perfume. With a well-practiced smile she said:

"I just want to thank you for your service to our country. I don't support the war, but I want you to know that I support our troops."

Brant's entire body tensed when he asked:

"So, how do you support the troops?"

"Well, I sent a care package to Soldiers' Angels last Christmas... and I have a yellow ribbon on my car... and..."

John turned to the flight attendant and whispered roughly:

"Ma'am, I know you are being nice, and you think that you are saying something that is politically correct, but please just go back to what you were doing before I embarrass myself and my son."

The flight attendant shook her head and walked off mumbling.

"Thanks, Dad. You handled that much better than I would have." Brant looked around, clearly annoyed.

John squeezed his arm and closed his eyes. Soon he seemed to be asleep. Brant looked at him and said softly:

"Dad, I know you and I have not spent a lot of time together, but I'd like to change that. Maybe it can help us both."

***

John heard Brant loud and clear. He felt dizzy and anxious. There were so many years of separation. Looking back, he realized that he had missed all the everyday running around, from scouts to sports to all the other things considered normal in raising a boy. He never connected with his boys, and he knew that this had a lot to do with the burden of overwhelming guilt he had felt all his life.

He was considered a war hero by most; yet he always felt like a fraud. Margarie knew him well, but she never knew his demons... and unfortunately, he never truly made a connection with anyone besides his wife. Years of reliving the experience of what happened on that one particular April day pushed him into bouts of depression.

He stood up and went after the flight attendant. When he came back from the front of the airplane, he sat down and handed his son two mini-bottles of whiskey and a glass. He pulled two more bottles out of his pocket and poured them into his own glass. Brant had never had a drink with his father, and could not hide his surprise.

"Brant, what I am about to tell you is what I've held so close to my soul for over fifty years. I hope it will explain why I have failed our family over the years and help us both move on."

John dug in under the seat in front of him and pulled the Journal from his carry-on bag. Without thinking, he thumbed its leather strap in a well-established ritual. He looked around and in a low, deep voice he uttered:

"This, Son, has been my punishment. This Journal speaks from the grave... on every page, in great detail, a German soldier tells his wife of the dreams he has for her and the future of their family... He describes his love. My German is terrible, but the little I know and the help of a dictionary enabled me to decipher his thoughts. I've kept it hidden because I was ashamed and scared. The Journal has traveled with me to Korea and Vietnam, and I can tell you that I did things there not out of heroics... but in trying to wash away the stain on my honor. Many times, I put myself in harm's way because I thought that might make things right. All the awards I received in Korea and Vietnam may be embossed with "for bravery" on the certificates, but by rights, they should brand me as a coward. Every morning, I rise to have breakfast with Rudolf Haas, the man who wrote his life into this Journal. We talk often… he is a constant presence. He taught me what honor means."

John paused to compose himself, "I thought I could return the Journal after Korea. I requested to be stationed in Bamberg, Germany, like you are now. My plans were to track down Haas's family. He wrote about the beauty of the city, and how he wanted to raise his family there, walking along the banks of the river, in view of the Rathaus.

When I got there, I could not even bring myself to start the search. I felt his presence. I could hear his voice, on occasion, after a few dark beers at the Schlenkerla. After I met your mother, it seemed the voices disappeared. I never discussed the Journal. Even though my German was very poor, and your mom's was fluent, I never let her read even one page. How stupid to think I could hide from my conscience. The war took my youth, and meeting your mother gave me back some peace, and normalcy. She was in Germany as an exchange student finishing her degree when we met. I fell in love, so madly in love with her and, even though she was much younger than I was, we had a lot in common. Oh, I am rambling… I'll get on with the real story."

Hidden Wounds: A Soldier's Burden

CAUCASUS (OCTOBER 1942)

"In the Soviet army it takes more courage to retreat than advance."

JOSEPH STALIN

The oil-stained map revealed only the main roads. Rudolf Haas squinted his eyes and leaned closer to view the crumpled piece of paper. The young German officer tried to see if there were any markings he might have missed. The rocky road caused him to hit his forehead on the edge of the turret, and with that one thump he was back in the present. He swore loudly, dropped the map, and raised his torso out of the turret of his Panzer IV. The headset crackled...

"Rudi, are you alright?"

The tank's driver, Hans Beck, was one of the best in the battalion and an uncharacteristically caring Nazi.

"Watch how you drive, *Grossmutter*," admonished Rudolf, "and call me *Leutnant* on the radio."

The dust rose around the column of tanks as they slowly clanked their way up the slope along with the infantry. The gorge was magnificent. Rudolf's mind drifted again, to his home. The fir forests, the vertical cliffs and the snowcapped Elbrus reminded him of the Transylvanian Alps of his childhood. The city of Nalchik, on the other hand, was not his beloved Hermannnstadt, but rather a motley collection of grey, government buildings blended with low houses, dotted with small windows and narrow doors. Nalchik looked every bit as unappealing as the globs of buckwheat porridge the Russians ate. Large flags emblazoned with swastikas shared the walls with discolored and peeling Soviet paintings depicting muscular factory workers wielding huge hammers. Loud speakers greeted the creeping column with German songs and messages in Russian urging the locals to cooperate with their "liberators." The city had been captured two days earlier in a strike that combined Romanian mountain troops with German tank and air support. In order to secure their hard-won gains, Haas's platoon and a company of Romanian infantry moved south to mop up the Soviets who might have escaped to the mountains.

* * *

Rudolf Haas was born and raised in a Lutheran family of Transylvanian Saxons. Rudolf always missed his childhood hometown of Hermannnstadt, after his father, infatuated with Nazism, moved the family from Romania to Germany in 1936. Hermannnstadt, or Sibiu as the Romanians called it, felt like a cozy nest to Rudolf. He loved to roam its narrow cobblestone alleys and sneak into the towers of the old city's walls where he and his friends would stage mock fights and pretend to fight off some fearsome Oriental invader. The city dwellers spoke three languages, but Romanian was the *lingua franca*. That detail drove Rudolf's father into long and angry ramblings about the German "founders of the city," and their declining influence in the Romanian kingdom.

Rudolf did not care. When he was not engaged in fencing with wooden swords or practicing bicycle stunts, he liked to read everything he could get his hands on. His favorite author was Jules Verne, followed closely by Alexandre Dumas. Rudolf's exceptional memory helped him to get high grades with very little effort. High grades afforded the prime benefit of keeping his parents off his back. Every year, he waited impatiently for the summer, when he spent most of the time at his mother's parents' place. Far from father's strict rules, Rudolf went hunting with Grandpa, gorged on Grandma's sweets, stayed up late watching the stars, and engaged in ridiculous peacocking to catch the attentions of the neighborhood girls.

At the time of the economic crisis that swept the world,

Rudolf's father came close to losing his job. Instead of being thankful for remaining employed, Haas Sr. exploded with rage and vowed to move where "German order and honesty still rule." The move took everyone by surprise and chagrined Rudolf. The family sold everything and moved to a small Bavarian city.

In Germany, Rudolf remained an avid reader whose biggest pleasure was to immerse himself in a dusty library for hours. At his father's insistence, he joined some athletic clubs and did rather well. Rudolf already spoke Hungarian and Romanian fluently and applied himself with passion to the mastery of English and French. His father had always refused to speak anything other than German and considered Rudolf's language skills redundant. The start of the war found Rudolf enrolled as a geology student in Heidelberg. Drafted into the Wehrmacht, the young Haas ended up unexpectedly in a tank outfit not long after his conscription.

Tank crew members were usually selected for their short stature; one rule not followed in Rudolf's case. At every formation, he stuck out like a sore thumb given his height. In basic training, an old Sergeant declared that any tank formation lucky enough to have an asset like Haas won't need a scout platoon, as the lanky Saxon would be capable of seeing far enough.

Haas, the soldier, missed campaigning in Poland and France, but he fought in Russia from the first day. Quite indifferent towards the Nazis, he was, nevertheless, a staunch believer in Germany's "Just Cause". The crew loved him for his mild manner and good humor. His rank progression was faster than he could have imagined. Through an ironic and surprising turn of events, his tank commander got a bullet in his mouth while explaining to a skeptical crew why the Bolsheviks are such poor marksmen. His college education made Haas the natural choice as the next tank commander. When his Lieutenant died during the siege of Sevastopol, Haas, still an *Unteroffizier*, became the acting platoon commander. Several months later, he received his battlefield commission during the second battle for Kharkov.

***

Now, the *Oberkommando der Wehrmacht*, as per Hitler's directive, aimed for Baku and the Caspian oil fields. The German armored and motorized divisions pushed back the Soviets and looked poised to cross the Volga at Stalingrad and occupy the Caucasus region in its entirety.

Rudolf Haas loved his armored machines. Most of the *Panzerkampfwagen IV* in the division got an upgraded main gun as part of the preparations for Operation *Edelweiss*. Finally, Haas's platoon had the tools to reply in kind to those pesky T-34s. All the German tankers loathed those rugged Russian tanks. Very tough to destroy because of the sloped armor, the T-34 was fast with wide tracks capable of moving on snow or in sludge during the dreaded *rasputitsa*, the season of the muddy roads.

Luckily, as Haas soon discovered, the Russians did not use radio sets in their tanks, and their tactics were quite poor. The German tanks, slower and with inferior guns, had somehow bested their Russian opponents so far.

As his column exited the gorge and neared a ridge, Haas thought that during the last month he had met very few enemy tanks.

"Maybe they ran out of them," he thought wishfully.

The convoy stopped, and Haas jumped down to discuss their plan with the infantry commander. The Romanians decided to stop on the ridge and dig in. Rudolf could find no reason to push deeper into the mountains, so he gladly agreed to halt and rest. While the infantry was cutting trees and digging trenches, Haas ordered his men to camouflage their vehicles. This was no tank-suitable terrain, and he had not seen a Soviet plane in weeks, but he didn't want to take any chances. He left Beck in charge and went off to survey the road ahead.

The ridge was heavily forested and steeper on the southern side. Taller ridges to the south were rockier and separated by deep, dark green valleys. The road zigzagged all the way down to a foamy stream, and then climbed again like a tan-colored snake in the lush evergreen forest.

"Nice blocking position," he heard in broken German behind him.

He turned around to face the infantry Captain.

"*Da, domnule Capitan,*" Rudolf Haas said quickly in Romanian, and waited with a poker face for his ally's reaction.

It was always entertaining for Haas to analyze the initial shock of the Hungarians or the Romanians when he spoke their language. This time was no different. The Captain's jaw dropped. The infantryman admitted with a surprised and embarrassed smile,

"Your Romanian is far better than my German."

That night, the tank crewmembers exchanged rations with the infantrymen and slept close to their vehicles to take comfort from the warm engines. As the Russians did not seem to be lurking about, Haas planned to return to Nalchik in the morning to refuel and to get ready for a new mission. The infantry Captain raised no objections as he dubbed his position "tank proof."

Haas woke up in the morning with a slight headache and chills. The air was cold and crisp. A thick white mist covered the valleys, making the peaks look like ships on a foam-capped sea. Sipping a hot ersatz coffee, Haas briefed his men and prepared the convoy for the road back. There were only five tanks and a beat-up Czech truck loaded with empty fuel pods. With no infantry marching along, Haas expected a short and uneventful ride back, so he took the lead position and put the fuel truck second.

Still bothered by the headache and hopeful that he was not catching a cold, he lowered himself into his machine and signaled Beck to drive. The rest of the column followed, and they were soon engulfed in the moist, thick fog. Visibility dropped, and Haas kicked himself for leaving so early. Neither willing to wait for the mist to go away nor to turn back, Haas slowed the convoy down to a crawl and ordered all the vehicles to keep visual contact.

Nobody heard the first shot, but Haas processed that something crazy had happened when the fuel truck missed a sharp turn and drove straight into the precipice. The high pitch of bullets hitting the armor plates forced him to drop down inside the turret and close the hatch.

"Don't stop Beck," he yelled, and then he turned the turret to look for the enemy.

The gunner announced,

"Visibility less than fifty meters."

Haas acknowledged this fact with an expletive. All of his tanks had five-man crews, and Haas determined that all of them would make it out. Because of the mist, the convoy could not move faster, so Haas slowed it even more and reduced the intervals. Praying that the Soviets lacked time to emplace mines, the Germans plodded ahead. As long as they had a clear road, the danger of getting killed or trapped remained low. The Russian anti-tank rifles lacked the punch to stop a Panzer IV, and Haas assumed that the ambush squads were short of heavier equipment. After several minutes as long as hours, the fog started to get thinner and the Germans caught sight of Russians in brownish greatcoats milling on the eastern slope of the road. The tanks' machine guns started to hurl cutting scythes of lead into their midst and the advantage passed to the tankers. The Russian fire slackened as the tanks' gunners found their range. Soon the firefight died down. The view opened up. Haas could see ahead to Nalchik and to safety. The ugly city suddenly became a very appealing destination.

Haas went straight to his battalion headquarters.

"Sir, the Russian infantry is controlling the gorge. I lost two men."

The Battalion Commander calmly listened to Haas's report about the lost truck, then asked him bluntly:

"How soon after refueling can you head back?" Haas's jaw clenched. The question made him think to himself,

"The old man's got a screw loose."

Oberstleutnant Emil von Reimer came from a long line of Prussian *Junkers* and knew his trade. All his questions were hints that helped or doomed junior officers so Haas took his time to come up with an answer. Then it dawned on him: The Romanian infantry knew nothing about the Russians controlling the gorge behind them. With one question, von Reimer had shrewdly made him volunteer for a rescue mission.

After refueling and explaining to his perplexed crew that they had to go back, Haas made it to the Romanian headquarters and pleaded for infantry support. Eager to get their trapped company out, the Romanians sent one platoon of mountaineers. Haas had the infantry ride on top of his Panzers. The mountaineers dismounted at the entrance of the gorge. Haas held no illusions as to their meager force's ability to clear both sides of the road, but his goal was to punch a hole when going in and then to blast his way out, reinforced by the fire power of the isolated company.

The cold October sun was now shining brightly as Haas peered through his binoculars. The infantry platoon had a hard time trying to keep up with his tanks. The convoy crossed the ambush site, and Haas saw their old fuel truck wrecked in a deep gully full of boulders. Haas made a mental note of the position, even though he had determined that the driver could not have survived that fall. The Russians had apparently withdrawn, or they had just felt too weak to challenge the Panzers again. As they approached the gorge's higher end, the convoy encountered a road barricade made of boulders and trees.

"Here we go," Haas said over the radio, and then time froze.

Two loud explosions rocked their front armor plate. The seasoned crew knew them to be tank rounds.

"Reverse! Reverse!" Haas repeated, while he and the gunner scanned the wooded slope for enemy machines.

Haas tried to ignore the staccato of the Russian machine guns and forced himself to locate the Russian tanks. The small arms fire grew in intensity, a sign that the Romanians had joined in the fight. The tanks backed up almost to the first curve when another round cut down a slender pine tree right next to them. This time the gunner saw the muzzle flash and loudly announced:

"Enemy tank... two o'clock... five hundred meters."

Haas felt both relieved and anxious as he processed the new data. So there must be a way around the barricade if the Russian tank had the nerve to negotiate that steep slope.

"Let's greet Ivan with our new high-velocity 75mm gun," Haas said, and ordered the Panzer to return fire.

The first Soviet tank got hit immediately and put out of action. Haas suspected that other enemy tanks waited near the barricade, so he cautiously pushed forward again. The gunner discovered the second tank as it emerged from the forest on the left between two huge boulders. Haas waited for it to come out in the open, as he intended to keep that route open for his convoy, and then their accurate fire scored another kill.

"Follow me and don't get stuck," he broadcast to the rest of his tanks, and then he plunged through the forest.

Once they passed the barricade, the Germans swerved back on the road. They surprised and disabled another Russian tank as they again pushed forward. Returning their attention to the Soviet infantry, the tanks fired their machine guns and occasionally a high explosive shell that soon silenced those Russians who lacked the decency to stay low and hold their fire.

Haas did not wait for the Romanian platoon, as he did not intend to allow the Russians time to regroup. The Soviet tanks came on the road through the "tank proof" position, so the mountaineers' defense had been breached. Haas's assumption proved correct. The ridge and its surroundings appeared engulfed in smoke and explosions. Soviet mortars had zeroed in on the Romanians and the Russian infantry had them surrounded. The Germans went in with the full fire of their guns, surprising the Russians so that the ones caught on the north side of the ridge either died or fled.

When they caught sight of the Panzers, the Russians on the south side joined the contagious rout. Haas moved quickly to take advantage of the lull in the fight. Gathering a handful of dazed survivors, Haas ordered them to triage their wounded and place them on stretchers. They were to leave the dead.

He found the Romanian Captain in a shallow foxhole. The man had multiple wounds and had most likely bled to death. Haas checked the Captain's pockets and took out his wallet. Inside he found cash and paper, and a small orthodox icon. On the back of the icon, someone had glued a photo with an impossibly beautiful woman holding a little boy. Both looked very happy. On the bottom of the photo was written "We love you" in neat cursive. Haas put the wallet back, but on an impulse kept the icon. Two Romanians came and took the Captain's body and placed him on a stretcher. Haas allowed them to ignore his orders. The dead Captain deserved a marked grave.

On the south side of the ridge Haas discovered the slope covered with dead Russians. He gaped at the evidence of persistence of the Russians to attack uphill and their willingness to take on horrific losses. The Germans estimated that the Russians lost half a battalion in their effort to overrun the Romanians. They had almost succeeded. Haas sent off the surviving Romanians on foot with their wounded. His tanks then formed a rear guard. By now the platoon that fought in the gorge made it to the ridge and joined their comrades in carrying the stretchers. The German tanks protected them all the way to Nalchik. For saving the besieged company, the Romanian brigade commander proposed that Rudolf Haas get an award and, to express his gratitude further, invited him and von Reimer to dinner. Haas fell asleep during the appetizers.

***

In the morning, a telegram from his mother announced his father's death. His request for leave was denied. Haas spent the rest of the day writing letters and making financial arrangements to have part of his pay sent home.

FROZEN STEPPE

"In the worldly steppe, so mournful and endless..."

A. S. PUSHKIN

The drive through the snowstorm mercilessly pushed men and machines. The whole 1st Panzer Army was racing desperately towards Rostov. The remnants of the once mighty *Panzerarmee* were fighting for survival as the Soviets tightened their noose around Stalingrad.

Haas and his men had two sleepless nights. Their battalion formed the vanguard of the battered German convoy. The Russians, eager to trap more German formations, kept erecting blocking positions in their path. Haas felt numb and the physical exhaustion made him almost detached. He pushed himself back in the game and forced his burning eyes to scan the whiteout. Haas knew that his men would not give up as long as their leader appeared to be in control. His platoon had only two tanks left. The others remained where they were halted, destroyed or abandoned, somewhere on the vast Russian steppe.

"1st Platoon move ahead and scout the village." The radio came to life.

Haas's two Panzers passed the rest of the convoy and headed west into the blizzard. They could barely glimpse the desolate village with its low huts covered in snow. They discovered the Russians too late. The Soviet tanks were dug in and clearly aware of the Panzers' presence. The T-34s opened fire. Haas's tank got hit in its tracks and was immobilized. The other German Panzer blew up in a horrendous explosion. Before Haas's gunner could return fire, the Russians hit them again. Smoke filled the tank compartments.

"Get out and try to make it back to the convoy on foot!" Rudolf Haas yelled as he opened the hatch.

Tracers lunged towards them from the village. The gunner got hit in the neck and slumped into a pool of blood. Haas tried to lift him but Beck pulled him away.

"He is dead Rudi… leave him."

The burning tanks illuminated the snow with an eerie,

hot glow and made them perfect targets for the Russian machine guns. Gasping for air, the four Germans dashed for the friendly convoy. Haas knew that the rest of the convoy, warned by the Russians' presence, was making its way around the enemy, entrenched in the village. When the Russian tracers stopped flying, Haas paused and tried to orient by sound. If they could not find the convoy, then the next closest German troops were hundreds of kilometers west, in Kuban.

The howling wind felt like sandpaper on Haas's face. He estimated the outside temperature at minus 20 degrees Celsius. After an hour of marching what they desperately hoped was south, the small group grew increasingly alarmed. For the four exhausted men, the absence of the convoy spelled disaster.

"We missed the convoy. We are on our own," Haas said. "We must make it to Rostov-on-Don, or to Anapa, on the Black Sea shore."

After a short discussion, the group split up. Haas decided that in pairs they had a greater chance to avoid capture. He and Beck chose to try for Anapa while the rest of the crew headed for Rostov.

Several hours of walking in the numbing cold convinced Haas to seek shelter. He could hardly feel his toes and recognized it as one of the symptoms of frostbite. The short and chubby Beck had difficulty breathing and sounded like he had a bad case of asthma.

"What an odd pair we make," Haas thought, and despite the situation chuckled softly.

Rudolf Haas looked like a Nazi propaganda poster. Tall and blond, he had handsome features and piercing blue eyes, Haas looked every bit the Arian prototype of the "superior" German race. Hans Beck looked more like a fat gypsy, and not a pretty sight at that. Beck had a round head with huge ears, thin black hair, and a swarthy complexion.

He had no chin whatsoever, nor a neck. With his short limbs and an imposing pot belly, Beck looked more like an innkeeper than a soldier. For his part, Haas found Beck's National Socialist convictions amusing and repeatedly poked his driver for his not-so-Arian looks. Nevertheless, Haas knew that Beck was fearless and competent without being a fanatic. Looks can be deceiving.

Haas recalled an incident when they were both Sergeants. They got drunk while playing cards with some tough-looking grenadiers. A tanned, muscular infantryman took pleasure in sarcastically calling them delicate ladies.

Beck's reply was slurred and garbled:

"Have you ever hit your head on a slab of igneous, intrusive rock?"

"What the hell is that?"

"I don't remember, but my friend here told me once. Anyway, it is not good for your head," Beck concluded with a wink.

As often is the case with inebriated men, the inferred warning did not cool the situation.

The other soldier laughed and dared Beck:

"What are you going to do, roll over me?"

Everybody stared in disbelief at how Beck floored the infantryman with one swing.

After Haas pulled him out, Beck mumbled with a confused look:

"Remind me …what's an igneous, intrusive rock?"

"Granite, my friend… granite," Haas answered, laughing.

***

Morning came. The weather got worse.

Beck tried to quench his thirst by eating a bit of icy

snow, against the advice of Haas. The ice was so cold, it felt like it was burning his lips and tongue, worsening his dehydration. The wind picked up and blew icy pellets in their faces. Both lost any sense of time or direction. They stopped hundreds of times to look at their tracks and at the compass in a desperate effort to navigate a straight course.

When Haas heard a wolf's howl pierce the storm's rumbling sounds, he thought that his sleep deprivation was causing him to hallucinate. That hope was shattered when Beck started cursing. On both sides, just at the limit of their visual range, Beck pointed at several, dark, low silhouettes. Sensing their weakness, the wolf pack had singled them out as potential prey. For now the predators were keeping their distance, but they were shadowing them in a loose, horseshoe formation.

"Damn it, Rudi. I do not know if I prefer to be eaten by the wolves or burned up in a tank."

"If those are your only options, I pass."

Haas felt a sudden rage towards all this adversity. He pulled out his Luger and fired one shot towards the closest wolf. He missed, then he fired again. He missed yet again, but at least had the satisfaction of seeing the whole pack running.

"That's right, run you pansies. I'll EAT YOU if you don't!"

"Don't waste your energy, Rudi. Let's go…"

"If they come again, I'll make you a nice wolf-fur shawl, Hans."

"If we spend another night in the cold, they will be chewing our frozen bodies."

"No, they won't. Gosh, can't you think positively just for a bit?"

"Nope, the optimist side of my brain froze first."

Dusk came and the blizzard made way for a clear night sky. The snow-covered plane looked endless as the full moon and the stars shone down on it. The temperature dropped even more. Both men tried desperately to stay awake and walk. Tired, hungry and cold, they kept pushing west as fast as they were able. Around midnight, Haas felt he had had enough. His vision was now blurry and his eyelids were heavy. Haas dropped to his knees and slid into the depths of a deadly sleep. His last conscious thought had been that he had stopped feeling cold. Two sharp slaps woke him up. Beck stood over him, preparing to hit him again.

"How dare you to hit an officer you Nazi *Schwein!*" Haas yelled jokingly.

Beck helped him to his feet. Both men knew that falling asleep in the open on this snowy field equaled death.

"Don't you dare leave me here alone, Rudi," Beck said with a serious and determined look.

Despite his own pain, Beck showed genuine concern for Haas's welfare. The bitter cold gave Beck bloodshot eyes, a purple nose and ears full of cracks. The officer could not help but poke fun at his driver.

"If we find a village you better hide, Hans."

"Why is that?"

"Because you could give an old lady a heart attack the way you look right now."

Both men laughed, and then grimaced when their dry lips cracked.

They kept hobbling in a westerly direction. Even with a compass and a map, the Germans could not accurately establish their position. On that featureless plain, there were no trees or high ground to shoot an azimuth.

***

"Russians!" Beck whispered, as the two lone Germans immediately took a prone position.

A cavalry patrol appeared from nowhere and stumbled upon them. Though anachronistic, the Russians kept large formations of cavalry and employed them for reconnaissance missions or deep raids on German supply depots. The patrol got closer. Haas could now see about thirty fur-clad soldiers mounted on sturdy steppe horses. The Soviets reeked of cheap vodka and rancid fat. Most of them had flat Asian faces and reminded Haas of the Tatars of old. The Germans could not believe their luck when the Russians kept on going past them. The cavalrymen even crossed the Germans' foot tracks without paying any attention.

Their good fortune held again when Beck spotted a village. Crawling to within earshot, Haas and Beck did not move for half an hour, listening intently for any sign of danger. The adrenaline surge caused by the cavalry patrol warmed them up for a bit, and now they felt bold.

"Looks deserted," Haas said.

"I don't think we have any choice but to get inside one of those huts," Beck replied.

Soon, both fell asleep burrowed in lice-infested hay. It was heaven.

***

Rudolf Haas opened his eyes and stared at a pair of dirty boots. Those boots look quite warm, thought Haas.

"Heil Hitler," the Russian said mockingly, and knocked them both out with the rifle butt.

Minutes later, Haas found himself with his hands tied behind his back in front of another partisan, a husky, bearded Russian. The partisan yelled at him in atrocious German,

"What are you doing here, *fascist pig?*"

"Returning home from a short ski trip in Caucasus, Comrade."

The fist came heavy and fast. Haas dropped like a sack of potatoes. His head hit the wooden floor with a sickening thud. He forced himself to stay conscious and keep his composure. The partisans were a merciless lot and Haas knew that. They usually killed their prisoners on the spot; a favor returned in kind by the Germans.

Haas always imagined death on a battlefield, trading armor-piercing rounds with a faceless enemy in a red star-painted tank. Now he could predict with a high degree of certainty that the gruff partisan standing next to him planned their execution. The Russian turned his attention to Hans Beck. His interrogation technique consisted of thoroughly beating Beck while yelling the questions. The method proved counterproductive as Beck passed out before he could answer. An older partisan came and dragged the Germans behind a ruined house. The Russian searched them for valuables and found the orthodox icon. With a strange look on his face, the old man pulled out a pistol. Haas cringed in anticipation. The old Russian fired twice.

***

The bed had white crisp sheets and smelled clean. Rudolf Haas raised himself up on his pillow to have a better look at the nurse working on his bandages. His frostbitten toes looked like hell, but the doctor promised him that he'd keep them attached. Moving his attention from his feet to the nurse, Haas sighed quietly. The nurse looked up and smiled. Haas felt embarrassed; like a high school student caught staring at some cute teacher.

"*Fraulein* Carla, you look very fresh today," Haas

stammered and instantly regretted his choice of words.

"*Danke Herr Oberleutnant*, I will try to keep myself from spoiling," Carla laughed back.

She leaned over Haas and whispered softly,

"You can see me later if you wish."

That evening, Haas could not believe his good luck. Two weeks ago, in a God-forsaken village in Kuban, an old partisan spared his life. He and Hans Beck managed to hide in a ditch at the edge of the village until the partisans left, and then got picked up by a German patrol. Now, in a Crimean field hospital, Haas held the prettiest nurse in the world in his arms.

The next morning's news from the front tempered his cheerfulness. Another patient, a Captain from 6th Panzer Division who'd had his leg amputated, told the story of Manstein's failed relief attempt at Stalingrad. For the Germans trapped on the Volga, the Luftwaffe remained their sole supply of hope.

"Now is the middle of the winter, Ivan's best season. We will beat them again in the summer," the Captain concluded.

Haas doubted that.

DOUBTS AND HOPE

"We'll dream only happy dreams
Echoed by wind's song in the trees..."

M. EMINESCU

Stalingrad fell on February 2, 1943. One week later, Rudolf Haas received orders to report to a training battalion in Germany. To his surprise, he also received the German Cross in Gold and a month's leave. Haas knew that his mother was waiting for him in Germany, but he was content to spend the leave in Transylvania visiting his grandparents. The hospital commander gave in to the handsome Lieutenant's request and signed Carla's leave papers as well.

* * *

"So, you are going to train on the new Panther tanks?"

Rudolf turned to his neighbor and replied,

"My orders just say training instructor, sir. I do not know what that entails."

"But first we have four weeks of leave, and we are going to spend it in Romania," Carla said, laughing gleefully. "So gentlemen, please talk about something other than greasy tanks."

The Major smiled, then leaned back into his seat and looked out the train window. Major Schwartz wore a shabby uniform but Haas knew that nobody would dare to challenge him on that. The Major had the Knight's Cross on his collar and half of his face was severely scarred from burns. Haas liked Schwartz instantly and knew his interest in the new tanks would build an instant bond.

To Carla's chagrin the two officers continued to talk for hours about the war, tactics and weapons. Haas found Schwartz dangerously outspoken but very accurate and lucid in his analysis.

"German military intelligence is a joke!" Schwartz said emphatically. "They grossly underestimated the numbers of the Russian divisions and the quality of their equipment. I started the campaign with 37mm AT guns! Slingshots would have been more effective against Soviet armor. When we discovered that the 88mm anti-aircraft gun could destroy any Russian tank, we gave the 37mm slingshots to the Romanians to guard our flanks at Stalingrad. We might just as well have posted traffic signs on the Don with instructions for the Russians saying *Attack here with tanks.*"

"What worries me the most is the way Russians have learned from us. A few months ago, any German tank crewman knew how to lure the attacking Russian tanks into a line of anti-tank guns. Now Russians do the same to us. I lost most of my tanks when I stumbled onto a Russian anti-tank belt. They pulled their tanks back when we attacked. I followed and took my Battalion into a death zone."

Schwartz paused and his jaw muscles tensed. Haas recognized the pain of losing one's comrades. The Major's tale matched his own experiences but Haas tried a more optimistic approach.

"Maybe the new tanks will swing the momentum back in our favor, sir."

Schwartz kept silent. The train rumbled past a destroyed village. An old woman dressed in black from head to toe stared at the train with a blank look. Haas suddenly felt guilty.

"Our policy towards the civilians could not be more pigheaded." Schwartz blurted out again. "Eight months ago we were received as liberators in Ukraine. Our governance squandered any civilian goodwill by implementing brutal deportations and executions. Instead of gaining allies, the German policy in occupied Russia just swelled the partisan ranks. For anybody with common sense, we lost any chance to crush the Soviets. We need to negotiate peace while we still have a bargaining chip. Our *Fuehrer* should take a look at the world map and compare the tiny *Deutschland* with the combined size of the Anglo-American-Russian foes.

Germany took on the whole world and he expects to win."

Carla and Rudolf looked nervously at each other. That type of defeatist talk could be interpreted as treasonous. Schwartz noticed their predicament and laughed.

"Do not worry *Fraulein*, the *Gestapo* agents find Russia quite unpleasant… more unpleasant than the truth. And what can they do? Send me to the *Ostfront*? It takes courage to cut through the fog of deceit and propaganda that infests our lives."

Haas tended to agree with Schwartz but would never be so open with his convictions. Most of the Wehrmacht officers, including Haas, tolerated the National Socialist Party as the political power that restored the pride of the Germans. However, as war fortunes reversed, disappointment with the Nazis became widespread.

Rudolf Haas's distrust of National Socialism predated the war. Raised in a multi-ethnic Transylvanian city, Haas kept his pride in being a German without looking down on others. He felt quite uncomfortable with the official propaganda about the German race's superiority and hated, with a passion, the *SS Einsatzgruppen* that followed the front line units like ravens, preying on weak and defenseless civilians. He also feared the retribution awaiting the German people because of the actions of those fanatics. After Stalingrad, the odds against the Third Reich appeared daunting indeed. Nevertheless, Haas steeled his resolve to do his duty.

***

Rudolf Haas and Carla spent the next few weeks as in a dream. Hermannnstadt seemed untouched by the war. The young couple walked down the cobblestone streets, ate at cozy restaurants, went to concerts and to the theater.

Haas even attempted to teach Carla skiing on the northern slopes of the Carpathians. They stayed with Haas's grandparents on his mother's side, in an ancient Saxon house. Grandmother prepared their breakfast every morning. Carla could not believe the goodness of the warm bread with butter and rose hip jam.

"I think I could live here forever," she said while sipping a cup of hot milk in bed.

Carla hailed from Danzig. Her mother was Polish, but Carla kept that a secret. She laughed or smiled a lot, and filled any room with her positive energy. Coming from a staunch Catholic family, she was more devout than Haas. In Hermannnstadt, she developed a fascination for the Orthodox liturgy and its mysterious monotone Byzantine chants.

"Rudi, did you know that the Orthodox Cathedral is a smaller copy of Hagia Sophia in Istanbul?"

"I did not know this; I've never been to Turkey," Haas teased.

Carla put down her cup and pulled the pillows and the covers around her.

"I know why your grandparents are so happy... because they married and lived in this city... and ate this jam. I wish for eternity to be just like this morning."

Carla sighed and closed her eyes.

The soft-spoken Lieutenant could not agree more. He, too, had found the perfect moment of happiness, chatting with his beautiful lover in a room filled with the faint smell of quinces.

One day, while hiking high in the mountains, they spotted two large eagles gliding above the valley. Haas told Carla,

"They are Imperial Eagles. They mate only once and forever in their lifetime. Their partnership lasts until one dies."

"They are magnificent," Carla exclaimed with her

contagious enthusiasm. "Too bad we cannot fly," she said with a mischievous smile.

***

Grandfather took him aside that evening and told him abruptly, "You must do what is right and honorable and marry this girl. You are smarter than your old grandpa, and you went to higher schools in *Deutschland*, but you are still one of us, and we do things the proper way."

Haas had his flings in University; he always dismissed the idea of marriage as something far ahead in an uncertain future. He was still embarrassed to remember his first sexual experience. In Heidelberg, after a series of grueling exams, he got seriously drunk with several of his colleagues in an upscale tavern. The students, caught in the fever of the semester's finals, called those late parties 'memory erasers.' Haas convinced what he considered the best-looking female in that pub to spend the night with him. When he woke up the next morning and saw her in the sunlight, the only positive adjective that came to mind to describe his conquest was... tall. As she left, she asked that he never contact her again. Haas only felt relief and even more so when he found out that she was the wife of his mathematics professor. After that bizarre encounter, his romantic life could surely only improve. His sense of humor and good looks ensured him pleasant company, whenever he needed. However, he never felt emotionally involved.

This time was different. Spurred by his grandfather's advice, he toyed with the thought for a week, then bought a ring. Rudolf and Carla were married in a modest Orthodox chapel by a Catholic priest. Proudly standing behind them was Rudi's grandfather, who, although a Lutheran from birth, felt that the Catholic ceremony was a small price to pay for the happiness of his only grandson.

Rudolf Haas took leave from Carla on a crowded train platform.

"Be my strong *Adler*," were her farewell words to him. He felt madly in love and found this new emotion a strong reason to outlive the war. As Rudolf's train rolled west, the new Mrs. Haas headed east. They both had hopes as high as the blue skies.

Hidden Wounds: A Soldier's Burden

KURSK

"All in the valley of Death
Rode the six hundred."

LORD ALFRED TENNYSON

The training unit kept him for only three months, enough for Haas to get comfortable with the new Panther tank. The *Panzerkampfwagen V Panther* had many technical glitches but overall Haas considered it outstanding. The *Panzer V* had a great gun, good speed and lots of power. The German engineers learned from the Soviets and adopted sloped armor for the front plates.

In June 1943, Rudolf Haas reported to the 6th Panzer Division Headquarters in central Russia. The division workhorse remained the trusted Panzer IV as the Panthers could not be produced in sufficient quantity. Haas saw that the SS formations got an even more impressive weapon: the fearsome Tiger tank. The German High Command concentrated all the German armor, bolstered by the new tank models for a new summer offensive. The Soviet positions formed a salient in the German front at Kursk. The stage was set. A battle larger than anything else in history loomed ahead.

***

Rudolf Haas ran into Hans Beck while overseeing repairs for his battalion vehicles at a maintenance shop. Haas begged his commander to pull some strings and got Beck transferred to his outfit. As Haas got a company command, he put Beck, now a Sergeant First Class, in charge of a platoon.

The orders to move out came on the morning of July 5th. Hundreds of tanks and self-propelled guns, followed by half-tracks loaded with combat engineers moved forward with engines roaring. The impressive concentration of combat power surpassed everything Haas had previously witnessed. Above the ground armada, returning from a bombing mission, a formation of German He 111s tipped their wings in salute. Minutes later, other friendly planes flew in the opposite direction. Haas's gunner counted hundreds of dive bombers and escorting fighters flying north.

"This is awesome, Rudi," Haas heard in his earpiece. The excitement in Beck's voice was contagious. "We'll kick some Bolshevik butt!"

"Nobody and nothing can stop us, Hans," Haas replied. The rush of adrenaline, the mix of fear and expectation permeated every man in formation.

Haas resigned himself to Beck's lack of formality on the radio. Haas disliked rigid formalism, though he could be quite formal at times. He liked being called Rudi because only his grandparents and Carla called him so. His parents had always called him Rudolf.

Less than two kilometers from the starting point, several Panthers had stopped due to mechanical failures. One kilometer further up they hit the first Soviet gun emplacements. Softened by the bombers, the Russian crews could not withstand the concentrated firepower of the Panzers. 6th Division plowed forward. Then they hit the first minefield. A couple of explosions disabled more tanks. The attack column halted and the engineers went forward to clear a path. They had to repeat the procedure three times. Haas knew they still had to cross two rivers and began to question the realism of the timetable briefed by the Division Commander.

Slowly, the Germans pushed through successive mine belts and Soviet fortified positions. The depth of the defense amazed Haas. The Russians must have known our plans, he thought. Because of the stiff resistance, the 6th Panzer Division did not cross the Donets River until July 11th. After a week of battling through endless anti-tank belts and minefields, Haas rode the only Panther tank still operable.

Beck's platoon destroyed twenty-three Soviet tanks and several 76mm anti-tank guns, and had a close call with a Russian heavy tank, a KV-1. That monster knocked out three German tanks, when Beck decided to flank him. Beck's gunner fired three times, scoring hits but no penetration. The KV-1's turret rotated and Beck desperately fired a fourth time. The round jammed the KV's turret as the Russian tank turned towards the Panzer IV with the intention to ram it. Beck's driver tried to create distance when Rudolf Haas rushed to help in his Panther. Haas's gunner hurried and missed. After a slight correction, the second round blew up the KV's track. The Soviet machine started to spin. A third round set the enemy armor on fire. Two dazed survivors crawled out and both raised their hands.

"Hold your fire," Haas ordered.

Before he finished, the Russians died in a hail of machine gun bullets. Haas cursed and vented over the radio,

"I said hold your fire!!"

"The engineers killed them, Rudi. They are on a different net. And thank you for saving my ugly mug."

Beck's voice calmed him down. Rudolf Haas reflected that all his library readings about the war could not convey the brutality and the cruelty of young men sent to kill other young men. Half a year ago, one partisan chose to spare two wretched Germans in Kuban. Now, Haas felt guilty and remorseful that he could not protect those surrendering Russians. His mind drifted to an episode from his childhood when he came back home with a black eye. A notorious bully had stolen his lunch, and sucker-punched him. His father asked him to go back and give the aggressor two black eyes. As his father could be scarier than any bully, Haas went after the kid and hit him in the head with a brick. The bully spent the rest of the trimester in the hospital, and Haas got expelled from school and achieved legendary fame in his neighborhood. Despite the sudden popularity, Haas hated himself for the disproportionate retaliation.

That day, Haas stopped talking about his problems with his father or with anybody else. Haas determined that no one could manipulate his fears ever again. Fear makes monsters out of ordinary people, and that was the reason Haas never joined the Nazi party.

***

When the armored juggernaut reached open country, the Germans thought they had cracked the hard shell of the Soviet defense. Even with the attrition caused by the grinding, week-long battle, Haas shared his superiors' belief that the advance would resume and the German Panzers could trap several Russian armies with a fast and decisive maneuver once again.

Standing up chest high in his turret, Rudolf Haas saw the German bombers turning towards the column and waved his hand. A sixth sense told him to duck and slam the hatch. The bombs exploded with a thunderous, numbing roar, and shrapnel hit the Panther. With ears bleeding, a disoriented Haas fumbled to adjust his optics. The radio crackled with shouts and orders. His hatch opened from outside and Haas could barely hear Beck's yelling.

"Rudi, are you OK?"

Haas nodded and shouted, "Can't hear you Hans... Where is your man voice?"

Beck remained serious.

"Your ears may be fried Rudi. I see them both bleeding... The division staff got wiped out..."

Haas fought through the cloudy thoughts and lifted himself up. The freak mistake of two Luftwaffe pilots crippled the 6th Panzer. The division commander was killed, and most of the battalion commanders had died or suffered serious injuries. The friendly fire surprised the senior officers huddled around the command vehicle for their morning staff briefing. A Major assumed the command and sorted the mess out. The advance resumed and the tank engines roared again from idle to full power. The division's tanks increased their speed trying to reestablish contact with the SS corps who went ahead.

The Panther cleared a small terrain rise. Haas choked with horror.

"Back! Back!" The driver reversed briskly and the machine moved back violently.

"Enemy tanks ahead! Hundreds! Looks like a whole army!" Haas broadcasted quickly.

The Germans used the small fold in the terrain to spread out into two long, thin lines with their tanks positioned in front, followed by the half-tracks. The new acting Division Commander requested air support. On the radio, things went crazy. Haas tried to make sense of the chaos while keeping an eye on the small rise. He took a deep breath and grabbed the microphone.

"If the Russians did not see us, we are going to ambush them. Faster loading and less aiming, they will be on us in minutes."

Sleek dark shadows moved above.

"Now that's fast air support. Let's just hope that this time, the Luftwaffe sent in the guys who passed their vision exam."

"Maintain radio silence!" The Major's voice cut short Beck's wise-ass remarks.

"Forward! Stop on top of the ridge and fire!" The order came loud and clear. Haas thought it suicidal, but his training made him obey. He switched on the intercom and told his driver,

"Watch out for ramming! Let's send them packing!"

The attack caught the Russians by complete surprise. Hammered mercilessly from the air, they got stopped cold by a line of German tanks that appeared out of nowhere. Some Russian machines turned and fled. Some came forward, completely disoriented. The few that returned fire had to cope with experienced German crews who kept their tanks low on the reverse slope with only the turrets visible. The grassland filled with smoke, dust, and burning wrecks. Most of the Soviet vehicles carried external fuel containers. Even near misses transformed the T-34s into speeding torches hitting each other in erratically evasive movements. After several minutes, the German dive bombers expended their ammo and left. The German tanks kept pursuing what still remained a sizable Russian tank formation.

More planes appeared above. Haas thought perhaps the pilots felt guilty for that morning and now they were bending over backwards to help the tankers. He did not realize his mistake until the bombs started to fall among the Panzers.

"Russian bombers!" The radio blared the obvious update.

The pursued enemy tank formation now became a deadly threat. If they turned on the Germans the situation could be reversed. Reluctantly, the Major ordered the division back. Twenty-two destroyed German tanks remained in the no man's land. Most of their crews were lost as well. The Russians probably lost five times more.

That evening, they heard that the SS armor fought a huge tank battle at Prokhorovka. In spite of inflicting massive Soviet losses, the battle resulted in a stalemate. The order to withdraw came the next day. Haas did not talk with his men that night. Any German with any level of intelligence knew that the battle of the Kursk had been lost.

***

Less than two weeks after the battle, Haas's division had to rush south to fight off a Soviet counterstroke. A twist of fate prevented Haas from joining his men. The night before the move, he was summoned to the division headquarters where a clerk handed him an open envelope.

Haas could not believe what he was reading; the orders were clearly typed on parchment paper bearing the *Fuehrer's* letterhead. The adjutant who wrote them, whoever it was, tried to impress. Haas was in line to receive the Knight's Cross of the Iron Cross; a much higher award than he had already received. In the past, he had jokingly referred to his Iron Cross as an enemy marksmanship badge. Virtually anyone who spent extended time in combat had one on his uniform. However, the Knight's Cross was held in very high regard, and the news surprised him. Even with his healthy German roots, Haas's Romanian heritage irked the purist Nazis in the officer corps.

On top of everything else, Haas was selected to receive his award at the *Livadia* Palace outside of Simerfol. He had received instructions to arrive several days early. He had been invited to participate in a quail hunt and to attend a formal dining event that included representatives from every armed service. The affair was being organized by the Luftwaffe, a sure venue for plenty of pomp and propaganda.

***

As was the tendency with any self-respecting soldier, Haas milked the situation and arranged for his wife to be invited, too. He even received permission to go and pick her up two days in advance. Haas could see that Carla was both proud and uneasy. Only half-joking, she told him, "If I can't keep my composure with all those snobs that want to take a picture with you, I'll leave you with your trinkets."

Haas grinned when Carla hugged him tightly. "I promise I'll make funny faces when they take photos… Let's see them they try to use *that* for propaganda."

"That should do it," laughed Carla." Then we can spend most of our time together walking around the gardens of Livadia."

In no time, they were packed and ready for the train ride.

***

As they stepped off the train, a Volkswagen was waiting for them. A handsome Luftwaffe Lieutenant snapped a perfect "Heil Hitler" salute. Haas returned a lethargic "Heil", ignoring the Nazi etiquette.

"It is an honor to meet *Leutnant* Haas and the lovely *Frau* Haas. I am Lieutenant Straub and I have been assigned as your escort. Anything that you require- please let me know. This afternoon is the quail hunt and a special reception in your honor, organized by Colonel Straub, my father."

Haas could see Straub studying Carla with poorly-masked desire.

This was going to be a long weekend. Maybe bringing Carla into this snake pit was a bad idea, thought Haas.

As the leering continued, the urge to punch this rosy-faced and pampered fly-boy almost overwhelmed him. Haas quickly shook off the emotion. He knew that his career would not survive him beating one of the chosen ones.

Livadia Palace and the surrounding grounds offered a breathtaking view. Haas enjoyed seeing how Carla gripped his hand and gave him a smile that made everything alright.

How did I find her in all this chaos? he marveled.

In less than an hour, Haas was changed into hunting regalia and was whisked off to meet the rest of the guests. He could not help but compare them to a muster of peacocks. Everyone was standing around, hands on their hips, each trying to upstage the others– the "look-at-ME" body language was deafening. As Haas walked up to the group, he was met with a barrage of "Heil Hitlers". Clearly this was not the time to be obstinate and give a half-hearted effort – especially with all that brass around. He reflexively boomed 'HEIL HITLER!' and was quickly brought into the fold. The national password and enthusiasm worked, now to maintain it.

The hunt was on for the bountiful quail. Haas had already been given the terms of the contest. In the next hour, the team with the most quail would be given the honor of sitting at the head table with the *Feldmarschall* von Manstein. Most of the "hunters" were senior military officers and Nazi Party officials. All of them drooled at the opportunity to sit next to Eric von Manstein; even more so as it was rumored that Hermann Goering would be in attendance. After twenty minutes, Haas and another Army officer were up five. He had hunted all of his life and this was truly a walk in the park for him. Some of the other hunters had their own shotguns and custom-fitted hunting gear; neither was helping, and with every shot, Haas climbed the score card.

His companion, an older Major, caught Haas's gaze and smiled. Haas knew immediately the implied message. He approached Straub's small entourage. Lieutenant Straub was frantically shooting to increase his father's numbers. This was truly a sick game. Haas had the sensitivity to play it right.

"Sir, do you mind if I join your group? The rest of the

teams have three or four members and your team and mine have only two."

"Knock yourself out, *Leutnant*! For us pilots, it's easier to keep a gun barrel pointed in the right direction when it is attached to a plane." Colonel Straub smiled, masking his frustration.

The hour was up and the birds were counted. The day went to Colonel Straub with twenty. As the group dispersed, one pilot approached Haas, "Well played, Lieutenant. It is never easy to know who is 'supposed' to win. Colonel Straub no longer flies but he was a legend during the days of the Great War. I would be honored if you would join us at our table; it would be great to know who we are supporting on the ground. We are having a get-together with our ladies before the dinner. It will be mostly pilots, but you are welcome to come over and have a few drinks with us."

Haas accepted, and jumped in the car wondering what the night would bring. He had survived the hunt; now he needed to navigate around a friendly Luftwaffe crowd.

***

Everyone immediately turned to stare when he entered the pre-dinner reception. Before he could utter a greeting, Haas felt a hand on his shoulder.

"Friends, this is Rudolf Haas, one of our beloved tankers. He's giving us the honor of joining us for a couple of beers before the big show. He survived the hunt. I hope he agrees to share his war stories with us."

Haas recognized the pilot who introduced him as the man who had invited him earlier, but before he had a chance to respond, Colonel Karl Bodenschatz entered the room.

Immediately, all the men stood at attention. The

Colonel looked around and gestured to everyone to sit. Bodenschatz exuded pure authority and the group was awestruck at his presence. One of Goering's closest friends, the adjutant was clearly in the mood to drink with his airmen and brethren. After a few beers, everyone seemed to get more comfortable while Bodenschatz chatted with Colonel Straub. As he was leaving, Bodenschatz stopped next to Haas, leaned over and uttered in a low voice, "I am sorry for the friendly fire incident."

He followed this with a loud "Danke!" Haas's stature was instantly elevated among the flyers, and then Carla entered.

***

Every eye was on Carla as she approached Haas. He could see the leering of the pilots and the envy in their wives' eyes. Haas chuckled, stood, and took Carla's hand. They were the center of attention in a room that did not share attention well.

"My Darling, welcome to my personal hell. Can I get you something to drink?" Haas whispered.

Carla grinned and kept her eyes on Haas as he walked her to the bar. As they sat, a middle-aged woman approached.

"Mrs. Haas, I am Eva Straub, and I want to introduce you to a few of the wives. As you can imagine, we never expected to attend a reception in Russia. During this brief visit, we would like to know if we can help our frontline hospitals when we return home."

Haas turned and saw Carla being escorted from the table. As he sipped a bit of wine, the friendly pilot nudged him.

"I guess you are fitting in nicely. So, I take it there is more to the story than you giving up a few of your birds for

Old Straub. You either saved someone's ass or you are the *Fuehrer's* long lost nephew. No, don't tell me. I just want to enjoy the show; and by the way, your wife is stunning; you are one lucky bastard. Please, take no offense; it is a heartfelt compliment from one warrior to another."

***

All the speeches about the final victory made Haas sick. He suspected the speakers themselves did not believe their bombastic words. At least the Russians were promoted from *Untermenschen* to *Barbaren*. Even the most deluded Nazis felt it necessary to convey through semantics that Russia was stronger than expected. He stopped listening and searched the room for his wife.

It did not take long for Carla to win over the wives; she was absolutely brilliant. As they sat at the head table nodding politely to von Manstein, Haas looked over at her thinking that class was a trait that could not be taught, bought or bestowed. Yes, he truly was a lucky bastard.

NORMANDY

"If a man does his best, what else is there?"
GENERAL GEORGE S. PATTON

During the spring of 1944, Rudolf Haas assumed a company command in a new outfit, the 9th Panzer Division. The division was stationed on the Rhone Valley in southern France. Haas welcomed the move, as he used the transfer to finagle a whole month of leave. Carla could not take any time off, so he spent two weeks with her in Odessa, where her hospital was evacuated after Crimea was cut off by the Soviet advance. The front news ranged from bad to worse and Carla worried about Rudolf. She was delighted to hear about the transfer.

"You are going to take a break from this hell and see France at the same time, but stay away from the French girls; I hear that they are like the mermaids."

"What do you mean? They smell like fish?" Haas said with a serious look on his face. "I have to try that kind of seafood…" he laughed while Carla hit him with a pillow.

"You know what I mean… Once they lure you into their bed with their charm, you are hooked. And I am not in the mood to joke about it."

Carla sighed and let Rudolf kiss her. "You need to write me every day, Rudolf."

***

On the day Rudolf left, Carla cried. Her instinct warned her of something dark and evil. She did not say anything to Haas as she did not want to upset him. Carla admired the confidence with which Rudolf declared that the future was theirs to conquer, no matter which way the war went. He told her that as long as they kept their honor and humanity, even in defeat, life would go on. Germans will marry and have children. "The world will not stop because Germany loses another war." Carla wanted to believe him but her intuition was telling her that the world would be very different after *this* war.

Two months later, Carla knew that a new life had started to grow inside her. Elated and scared at the same time, she planned to write to Rudolf as soon as her shift was over. Before she could write her first line, a new batch of wounded came in from the front. The doctors worked through the night, amputating, extracting shrapnel and repairing broken human beings. Carla could not write a word, that night or the next as she labored to keep up with the flood of new patients. The front came closer. The artillery duels could be clearly heard and the flash of explosions lighted the horizon with a ghostly glare. The hospital commander ordered everybody to be prepared for any contingency in the event of a forced evacuation.

***

Rudolf Haas arrived at the headquarters of the new division in May 1944. He was in a terrible mood as news from the collapse of the German front in Ukraine reached even the official Nazi newspapers. He pushed on with the training. With a vengeance, he tuned up his company of Panthers and Panzer IVs to a high degree of responsiveness and marksmanship. His gunner asked him if he would like to have a mascot painted on his Panther.

"Yes," Haas said, "paint me an Imperial Eagle."

Haas liked the drawing so much he copied it onto the inside cover of his Journal. It was his bond with Carla.

When he finally got the official confirmation that his wife's medical unit was overrun, Haas felt powerless and angry. He blamed himself for not trying to get Carla transferred with him to Western Europe. Nevertheless, he kept all the anguish and guilt and self-blaming thoughts hidden. Haas felt responsible for his new company, as all the men looked at the new Captain transferred from the Eastern Front with hope and trust. Haas's feeling that he was serving an evil puppet master was damped down by the camaraderie and the attachment that he felt for these young Germans. Even if they were fighting a losing war, they deserved the best leadership he could produce. He pushed the pain and worries for Carla deep inside.

Let's lose the war first, thought Haas with self-defeat and sadness as his aching mind struggled to hope that she was safe somewhere, even in a POW camp, and that sooner, or later they would cross paths again.

***

The new company performed well in training considering the percentage of green tankers on their first assignment. The men obeyed and acted professionally, but with some reserve and without the confidence that Haas expected. As always, with a new commander the jury was still out, and Haas knew that. The real breakthrough with his new outfit came during their first rail movement.

A partially destroyed bridge stopped the battalion train out in the open. A German team of engineers was on site working. Around noon a single plane circled around at high altitude. Rudolf felt uneasy. He went to the engineers.

"How long?" he asked.

"Sixteen hours minimum... maybe more... sir," a very tired and grubby Sergeant answered.

Haas thanked him. He took out his binoculars and looked around. The broad river meandered in a flat open plain enclosed by rolling hills with forest patches and culti-vated fields. He went to the train commander, a Luftwaffe Major, and pleaded with him to move back to one of the tunnels. When the Major refused, Haas asked for permission to detrain his tanks.

"If you want to keep your men busy with this non-sense, knock yourself out," growled the annoyed Major.

Haas ordered the ramps installed. To detrain out in the field was tedious work. Under the amused and mocking looks of the other companies, Haas's men toiled to unload the steel monsters. Haas directed each vehicle to the nearest woods as soon as it was unloaded. When the anti-aircraft guns went into action, the only tank left unloaded was Haas's. He jumped in and yelled:

"Drive! Now!!"

"But sir, there is no ramp," whined the horrified driver.

"Drive you *dummkopf.* Drive or die!"

One plane took a direct hit from the train's flak, its *Flugzeugabwehr-Kanone,* and blew up in an orange ball. Three other planes dived in and took out the flak crews with their .50 caliber machine guns. The fighters made another wild pass, firing their machine guns, then soared high and turned. Haas watched in horror as the planes formed up to drop bombs and align their 20mm canons, methodically chewing up the defenseless train.

The driver closed his eyes and pushed the heavy Panther over the edge. They landed hard and the aftershock made them feel as if they were inside a huge, ringing church bell. Luckily, they did not roll over given the speed and trajectory at which they had left the blazing train.

The American fighters did not leave until they had exhausted their ammo. The only rail car platform left undamaged was the one carrying the train commander. The unfortunate Major suffered a shattering nervous breakdown. He never spoke with Haas again.

It was Rudolf Haas's first encounter with the deadly P38 Lightnings. It would not be the last. After that experience, the men worshiped their Captain. In their eyes, he could do no wrong.

***

The allies were crawling up in Italy, and Haas expected to see action there. However, in June, the Allies invaded Normandy. They broke through the coastal defenses of the overrated Atlantic Wall, but they were contained more or less in their beachhead for almost two months. Because Hitler refused to commit his armored units, 9th Panzer did not make it to the front until August. By then the battle was already lost.

Rudolf Haas and his men detrained and rolled straight into the fray as the Germans struggled to hold an escape avenue open for the units caught in the Falaise pocket. The Sherman tanks proved less of a menace than the Soviet armor and in any pure tank versus tank encounter the Panthers, Tigers and the German tank destroyers usually had the upper hand. However, the casualty rate became dangerously high. Conditioned to the swarm tactics employed by the Russians, Haas discovered painfully that fighting the Americans required a completely different approach. The war strategy of maneuvers that the Germans had mastered in Russia now had to be abandoned in favor of night movement and thorough camouflage during the day.

The Allies valued their manpower and rarely insisted on attack if it might cause them to take heavy casualties. Instead of the massive artillery preparations used by the Russians, the Allies used a deadly and omnipresent air power to pulverize any German unit, armored or light. The mass counterattacks, so widely employed before by the Panzer formations, became recipes for disaster as the Allied pilots strafed and bombed anything that moved. Haas witnessed a Tiger thrown around like a toy, when one five hundred pound bomb caught it in the open. Any patch of wood now became the Panzers' safest hideout and Haas made sure that his company had the thickest foliage above their machines.

On the night of August 13th, with the American Third Army closing in on Argentan, Rudolf Haas lead three Panthers through thick underbrush and past the American screening patrols. He intended to set up an ambush and snipe, with his main guns, at any convoy with reinforcements and supplies that the Allies might send forward. Strict radio discipline meant that the Germans had to keep up with each other in the dark. Haas found a spot at the edge of a dried creek, on a forested hill overlooking a road. By his estimation, they were five miles behind the forward Allied positions and that road could very well be one of the main supply routes employed by the Allied units in front of Argentan.

With the light of dawn came a convoy of Shermans and halftracks, followed by supply trucks that clogged the road. Haas could not see the end of the column, so he decided to hit hard and run. He broke radio silence and ordered, "Fire at will!"

The Panthers spewed out their lethal rounds. The tanks in the convoy turned their turrets scanning for their invisible foes. The Allied infantry jumped out of their carriers and fanned out on both sides of the road. Haas's guns kept firing and scoring hits almost every round. The Sherman tank crews figured out the Panzers' hideout and AP rounds started to bracket the Germans. The road was a blazing alley of wrecks when Haas stopped firing. He tried to anticipate the next Allied move. By now, he realized from the radio traffic that the column was a French outfit equipped with American hardware. When 105mm artillery rounds started to fall among the Panthers, Haas ordered:

"Let's go… keep inside the woods; I'll be the last tank."

Haas looked through his optics one more time as his driver backed up and turned. The explosion shook the tank and Haas felt all the air escape his lungs. The Panther slid sideways in the dry riverbed and the tracks spun furiously trying to get traction. Struggling for breath Haas yelled, "Stop! Turn off the engine."

The driver obeyed and the war machine stood silent. The air attack continued outside with the planes switching their unwanted attention to the other Panthers. After one long minute, Haas dared to crack open the hatch. He could not see anything but the river banks. The silence after the previous cacophony of explosions felt unreal. Haas pushed the hatch all the way open and jumped out. The Panther position worried him but the driver decided that he could maneuver one track and roll out in one piece.

Haas carefully crawled up on the steep bank and looked around. He could see one Panther smoking just fifty meters to his left. He assumed that the third one made it out alive. He cautiously approached the destroyed tank. The inside compartments were smoldering. The smell of burned metal mixed with the smell of burned flesh. Haas returned to his crew.

"Let's go!"

The tracks turned and the Panther eased its way sideways until both tracks churned into the soft riverbed. With the engine humming only a notch above idle, the driver pushed on, trying to find a way to exit.

"Just drive. Eventually, we will get out somewhere," Haas directed, as the tank started to pick up speed on the water-built highway. Half a mile later the left bank offered a gentler incline, and Haas decided to risk it.

"Step on it!"

With its engine revved up, the Panther sprung out of

the dry creek at high speed. They ended up in the middle of the road.

Instinctively, the gunner turned the turret. Haas stared at an American jeep driving straight towards them. The distraught driver came to a screeching halt at the last minute when he realized that the tank, with a blue eagle painted on its front, was not friendly. The gunner depressed the main gun. Haas immediately ordered, "Hold your fire!"

The American soldier desperately tried to back away, but he fumbled the clutch and killed the engine instead. As the Jeep sputtered and died Haas looked at the American. The driver, a young lanky lad, had an MP helmet and no weapon visible beside the belted pistol. Haas opened the hatch and ordered him in English:

"Move away from the vehicle!"

The American hesitated.

"Run!" Haas shouted.

He ordered his driver to approach the jeep slowly. Finally, the GI bolted into the woods and the tank crushed the jeep. To his gunner's interrogative stare, he said coldly, "You shoot one soldier and it will result in us getting hammered by more bombs. Think about the consequences!" Haas was tired of the senseless killing.

***

After the Allies sealed the Falaise pocket, the 9th Panzer escaped east with only five tanks left from the initial one hundred and fifty committed. France had to be abandoned, and the 9th Panzer retreated all the way to the Siegfried Line. The Germans ran so fast and far that the Allies could not keep up with them. The 9th Panzer used that breathing space to dig in around Aachen. Haas felt despondent and powerless. He asked himself again and again, *What's hap-*

pened to Carla? and *Why does Germany keep fighting?*

The news that Romania had left the Axis and turned against Germany made him ache with despair. Grinding all this in his mind brought him to the brink of exhaustion and prompted his commander to order him to take a week off. Haas slept through it.

WACHT AM RHEIN

"The quickest way of ending a war is to lose it."

GEORGE ORWELL

On December 16th, 1944, the Germans mustered their last reserves and launched a desperate offensive in the Ardennes. Deceptively named "Watch on the Rhine", the operation plan resembled the successful blitzkrieg maneuver that crushed France in 1940. Deftly, the attack took advantage of the winter weather temporarily, denying the Allies air superiority and masking the massive troop concentrations. The 9th Panzer Division, as part of the 5th Panzer Army, spearheaded the central thrust.

∗∗∗

Rudolf Haas stood up in the cold wintry air and looked through his binoculars for the 100th time. The snow-covered landscape masked the few narrow roads that were a challenge even in the summer time. Haas lead the column, and the responsibility made him nervous.

He recalled the briefing map with the objectives shown with red markings. Haas and other company commanders watched in disbelief as the briefing officer pointed towards Brussels and Antwerp as their final goal. Udo Weiss, a fellow Captain who befriended Haas during the retreat from France, leaned over and whispered, "I bet we won't make it to the Meuse River."

Haas did not answer right away. He figured since '43, that the powers that be in Germany had lost all their common sense and logic. After the briefing, he pulled Udo into a quiet corner and let some of his frustration out:

"… I bet they planned this on a map; calculating the time needed for a tank to drive at thirty kilometers per hour from here to Brussels. Even if we achieve surprise, to jam hundreds of heavy tanks into those narrow corridors while the enemy rules the sky is an insane idea. In 1940, we attacked in late spring against poorly led French infantry who lacked mobility. The air belonged to the Luftwaffe, and the French did not learn until too late to concentrate their armor. This time the Oberkommando der Wehrmacht expects the same results, in deep snow, and with all those American tank divisions somewhere on our left flank just waiting for us to give them an opportunity."

"Come on, can't be so bad," Weiss sneered. "We will run out of fuel before they can hit us. And if the weather clears up, their tanks won't shoot because their planes will take care of business."

They both burst out laughing. Several senior officers turned their heads with bemused looks. One of them said, "At least the morale is high."

Haas and Weiss laughed harder.

***

Later that day an SS Major approached Haas with an intriguing offer. Haas was tapped to join a secretive group of English-speaking Germans. Their mission: create chaos and confusion in the Allies' ranks and try to capture the Meuse river bridges. When Haas understood that he must wear an American uniform he flatly refused. The Major's face hardened, "May I ask why you are refusing this mission?"

Haas sensed the trap.

"My accent is horrible. I would jeopardize the entire operation. My best skills are to blast out enemy tanks. With regret, I must decline this honor."

"Well then... good luck in your tank fights *Hauptmann*...and this conversation never took place," the Major barked and waved him off.

Haas saluted, while conjuring his best military bearing, and left as fast as he could.

***

At first, Rudolf Haas could not believe the total surprise that his Panzers achieved.

We must have caught them sleeping, he thought, as he watched in disbelief, the long lines of American soldiers being marched back in captivity.

He strove to keep moving forward, bypassing any strongly defended positions. Even Weiss's fuel prediction did not come true, as they kept rolling a couple of days more on captured American fuel. The timetable, however, fell apart as tough pockets of resistance, especially at the road junction to the city of Bastogne, channeled all the German convoys into a traffic jam from hell. To top this, the sky cleared and the Allied fighter bombers took their vengeance on the Germans after swamping the feeble Luftwaffe air cover.

Both sides fought through Christmas Eve, surrounded by evergreen trees laden with snow. Lack of fuel and ammo shortages stopped any forward movement 10 kilometers from the Meuse River crossing at the French city of Givet.

On Christmas night, Udo Weiss joined Haas at a cold dinner. Several tankers were singing *Oh Tannenbaum* in the background. Haas's mind wandered to the last Christmas spent in *Hermannnstadt*. He indulged in that fuzzy nostalgia when he smiled sadly and said, "Merry Christmas, Udo… and your prediction came true… we did not make it to the Meuse."

"Well, I hate to be right… and now we are stuck here. I got no fuel left. My ammo is almost gone, and our artillery is apparently stuck in a traffic jam, God knows where."

Weiss pulled out a crumpled letter and announced:

"I got my Christmas present Rudi… I am going to be a father. As long as I make it out of here alive, I've won my battle."

Haas hurried to congratulate his friend.

"We are both going to make it out, and our men too… on foot if necessary," Haas spoke out loud. He thought with a tinge of envy: "Carla could have written such a letter if …"

"Did you ever think of surrendering … to the Americans?" Udo asked while chewing some canned meat.

Haas sighed.

"I don't want to go over and surrender… I would feel like a deserter… but I wouldn't lose men unnecessarily either… if they trap us, I would gladly give up."

Haas regretted instantly being so open. Weiss looked like a nice fellow, but loyalties could be deceiving. To his surprise Udo answered, "I would give up now if I could. Even so, I agree with you. Better to wait for the right time. After this mess even our *Fuehrer* may sue for peace."

"Don't bet on that," Haas blurted out.

On December 30th, the 9th Panzer withstood a sharp blow right at the tip of the salient carved in the Allied lines. The American counterstroke made the division reel back. Several Tiger tanks had to support the Panzer IVs and the Panthers just so they could hold the precarious line of defense. The 9th Panzer dug in, hoping that the supplies and reinforcements would catch up.

The following week, bad news piled up. In Bastogne, the US paratroopers stood fast and the American pressure in the South used up all the German reserves. The orders to pull back came in January 1945, just as the division crumbled under constant pressure from several Allied units. The Tigers guarded the pull-back, sniping at the enemy armor from long range. The Sherman crews dreaded the heavily armored Tigers with their long 88s and avoided them whenever possible. Unfortunately, for the Germans, the British and American pilots were drawn by the big machines like bees to honey. All sorts of aircraft mercilessly pounded the exhausted crews. Most of the remaining tanks had to be abandoned for lack of fuel. Paradoxically, once on foot, the withdrawal quickened as the roads became less clogged.

***

They made it out. Tired and dirty, dodging strafing fighter bombers and leaving most of the heavy equipment behind, Weiss, Haas and the other survivors straggled back to the German lines.

"At the dawn of the fifth year of war, in the minds of many, the burning question remained: Hitler gambled his last card and lost... now, what?"

Haas underlined that question in his Journal.

THE LAST DAYS

"Hardly had I thought I should learn to perish."

M. EMINESCU

During the last days of March 1945, the remnants of the 9th Panzer fell back in the small city of Siegburg. The German counterattack at Remagen Bridge failed in the face of impossible odds. The Americans and the British armored divisions were racing to close a steel ring around the Ruhr, and no German unit could stop that.

Rudolf Haas looked tearfully at his exhausted men and quietly thought that their efforts deserved better. Shortages of fuel and ammo made Haas conclude that Siegburg could be their last stand. He intended to look for Weiss and to coordinate a plan with him to defend outside the populated area and thereby avoid civilian casualties. Once in the city, he headed towards the city hall to request some food and shelter for his tankers. Walking fast and distracted by his thoughts, he failed to notice anything unusual until his gunner put a hand on his shoulder and pointed skyward. A corpse in German uniform dangled in the afternoon sun, the thin rope had cut deep into his neck. On the dead man's chest, a square piece of white cardboard had a single word: "deserter."

Haas needed a few seconds to recognize that the condemned man was one of his Lieutenants. Two days earlier, that unfortunate kid had suffered a nervous breakdown when a British Typhoon strafed his tank. Haas had seen the airplane coming low and spitting death with all four 20mm guns. One of the rounds hit the driver, severing his head and spraying the Lieutenant with blood and brain matter. Haas found his subordinate in shock and out of the fight, so he sent him back as a liaison with the civilian authority in Siegburg. Obviously, the powers that be in Siegburg did not need any liaison officers.

Pain and rage overtook Rudolf Haas. He went into the half-destroyed city hall and yelled at the first civilian he met, "Who executed my soldier?!"

Before the man could answer, a sweaty Volkssturm

Sergeant ran to Haas and saluted:

"The military court condemned and executed that worthless deserter, sir. They are convening upstairs."

Haas turned and punched the middle-aged Sergeant square in the nose. The man fell in pain and covered his face with his hands.

Alerted by the commotion, several tankers came and saw the dead Lieutenant hanging in front of the city hall. Weiss and some of his troops came in as well.

Haas looked at Weiss and said one word, "Upstairs."

Jumping two stairs at a time the tankers busted the door open. The "military court" had no military members, just some local Nazi officials with a Gestapo officer in charge. They were about to read a guilty verdict in another desertion case of a teenager from the *Hitlerjugend*.

The court president stood up and ordered Haas and his men out of the room.

"I am the one in charge here today," Haas barked back while his men seized the "court" members and brought them outside.

The tankers hanged the Gestapo man and no one in their chain of command or in the community dared to challenge them.

* * *

In the next week, the beleaguered Germans shot most of their remaining AP and HE rounds in the effort to repulse probing attacks from the south. Convinced that the fighting would be over in a matter of days, Haas instructed his men to remain together and maintain order when they would inevitably become POWs.

"Hold on a little more," he urged them.

When his battalion adjutant came to Haas and asked

to discuss "an important matter," Haas expected that the day of surrender had come. Surprisingly, the Major told him that he intended to break through the Allied lines and rejoin the German units still fighting in the east. An incensed Haas told him flatly, "Good luck, Sir. You can take all my tanks but none of my men."

"That sounds like defeatism, Haas. I could!"

Something in Haas' eyes made the adjutant stop mid-sentence.

"Sir, I will fire all my ammo to create a diversion and support your breakthrough, just to let you know, my men and I have had it. We've lost the war... Why this nonsense of keeping on fighting? I do not want to fight until the enemy erases Germany from the map."

The Major looked at Haas and admitted, "You are a man of honor, Rudolf. Nevertheless, I do not want to give up yet. The *Fuehrer* asked us to do our duty to the end. Heil Hitler!"

Haas deliberately answered the Nazi salute with a military salute. The Major frowned.

"You know that the military salute has been outlawed since the *Fuehrer's* assassination attempt. You're a hard-headed Transylvanian Saxon, Haas."

"No, Sir. I am just a German soldier fed up with Nazis."

The Major made it through. Haas admired that feat as a soldier, but deplored the uselessness of it. On April 13th, Haas and Weiss took a vehicle, a large white flag and drove towards the American outposts. That morning, Rudolf Haas wrote the last entry in his Journal:

"Today is the day I dreaded. I am tired and sad and empty. I feel no shame in defeat, rather joy that I survived. I may be selfish, but now that the war is over, I care less about Germany and more about Carla. If there is a God, she is safe somewhere, and maybe we will get a second chance at life."

***

John closed the Journal and carefully buttoned back the leather strap. His wrinkled hands were steady as he had already made up his mind. Smiling sadly he turned to Brant, "Son, when Rudolf Haas decided to spare that driver in Normandy, he saved my life. I was that scared kid. Unfortunately, I was not man enough to return the favor. Your father's story is not as unblemished as that of Haas. ... It all started in the English countryside..."

***

John Dougall recalled the first time he met McGee in England. As John walked into the tent, he snapped to attention and saluted the stocky Sergeant.

"Private Dougall reporting for duty, Sir."

"First of all, I am a Sergeant. I work for living, and if you ever salute me again, I will chop your arm off and feed it to you. Sit down. You are going to be my new driver, and you have a lot to learn. I have been in this unit since they formed it, so just listen and learn. If I don't tell you to do it, then don't do it...understand?"

John's first impression of Sergeant Mac was that of a rough man who knew his job. As they prepared to cross the channel, he felt that as long as he listened to McGee, he was going to be alright... The Sergeant would take care of his men.

During the invasion, after the infantry secured the beach and the logistical lines were taking shape, the MPs had to man key checkpoints along the supply routes. They operated in small teams, directing the supply trucks to the forward edge of the battlefield. A key part of their mission was straggler control. They got soldiers reunited with their units, guided displaced civilians, and processed enemy prisoners of war. Several weeks after the D-Day landing, John's company deployed just south of Cherbourg. McGee had a checkpoint set up right across from a café. John heard him threatening the owners to keep the hot coffee and food coming, or he would personally burn down their café.

"Sergeant Mac, why are you talking to them like that? Aren't we here to liberate them?"

"Don't be stupid Dougall. They know I'm not serious, and besides these surrendering monkeys owe us more than chow… These are a bunch of Nazi-loving, Vichy swine and I am doing them a favor by being their customer."

"Monsieur, would you like some more coffee?"

Dougall turned around and saw a middle-aged man holding a carafe and a cup and saucer. The cup was clicking against the saucer as the man's hands trembled.

"No thanks Froggy," McGee grinned and headed into the café.

Private Jeffcoat, the newest man on their team walked away from the Browning .30 caliber machine gun and quickly grabbed the cup. He drank it down and then smashed it against the wall hoping to get a reaction from the café owner. Jeffcoat was a Sergeant McGee clone. Dougall found it all scary and sickening.

"Jeff, hey, I am going to check to see if Sergeant Mac is alright."

As John Dougall walked into the café, he could see the patrons avoiding eye contact and heard commotion from the kitchen. He stepped in. The barrel-chested Sergeant was holding a girl, trying to kiss her on the neck.

"Sergeant Mac, what's going on?"

The young woman broke free and ran.

"Dougall, what the hell are you doing away from the truck?"

"I am sorry Sergeant; we just got a call from higher to move to the next checkpoint."

John fought to control his emotions as he was lying through his teeth. All he wanted was to get the Sergeant away from these civilians. As they walked to the truck, McGee started ranting about the French whores and how they must have loved having the Nazis crawl over them.

"I should just burn this place down and show them that they can't play both sides."

John glanced at Jeffcoat and quickly grabbed the radio.

"Roger. Copy last. We are en route to TCP two zero."

"Dougall, what are you doing? The radio is silent..."

"Jeffcoat, you need to get your ears checked. That's why I can't leave you alone more than a second. You never hear the radio – you're always daydreaming about goats, sheep or whatever it is that you've got back on that farm of yours."

Over the next few months things got a little better. They were attached to a larger tank outfit and McGee appeared to be on his best behavior. Everything went south during the Battle of the Bulge when McGee received the news about his brother's death at Malmedy. McGee vowed to kill any German he caught. His first chance to carry out his threat came after they crossed the Rhine.

At Remagen, they found an injured German hiding in

a ditch by one of the American checkpoints. McGee simply walked over to the wounded man, put a gun to his head and pulled the trigger - the metallic click caused the German to wet himself. McGee started laughing so hard that he had to sit down. He kept saying, "Did you see that? Did you see that? Now *that* is funny! Ok guys; now we are going to do it for real…"

As McGee prepared to dispatch the German, a jeep crested the hill leading down to the checkpoint. The truck stopped and an infantry Major got out.

"What the hell are you doing, Sergeant?"

"Sir, this German was low crawling up to our checkpoint; we discovered him and I was just getting ready to take him into custody so we could send him back to the rear for interrogation."

"Sergeant, are you sure this guy was trying to ambush you? He doesn't have a weapon, and from his wounds I am not sure he could crawl anywhere. I'll take him back to the rear."

The Major looked over at Dougall.

"Son, do you know what an accessory is?"

"Yes, Sir!"

"Then you don't have an excuse." The Major turned to McGee.

"Sergeant, I am going to report what I saw. Get your stuff together and report back to the command post."

After the officer left, McGee walked over to Dougall and smacked him in the side of the head so hard that it knocked him off his feet. McGee stood over him with pure rage in his eyes.

"Stick to my story… That bullet has a destiny… It is going to find its way into someone's head… I don't care if it's yours."

As they drove back, John pondered his chances of turning in McGee. If McGee kills a prisoner, then he is an accomplice, as the Major pointed out; if he ratted out McGee and the slippery Sergeant gets away with just a verbal scolding…

The company commander was waiting outside the command post.

"Hey, Mac what is this BS about you mistreating a prisoner? I got some Major going off to the battalion commander about how the MPs are out of control. He thinks you were going to finish off that Nazi right there in the ditch."

McGee produced his story while John sat quietly in the driver seat.

"OK, I knew I could count on you to do what's right. I have already talked to the old man so don't worry about it. Remember Sergeant, perception is reality; watch out how your actions can be interpreted. The last thing I need right now is a field grade sticking his nose in my company."

McGee saluted and that was the end of it. What the Captain didn't realize is that he had just given the green light to Sergeant McGee to exact his own personal kind of justice.

* * *

"Hey guys, check this out… Can you believe it? Here comes another bunch of Nazi cowards with their white flag."

McGee walked to the radioman telling him not to call it in. Jeffcoat trained his .30 caliber on the vehicle as it approached the checkpoint.

"Jeff, do you want to fire them up now or when they get here? This is going to be like shooting fish in a barrel."

"Sergeant Mac, they are surrendering. We can't fire on them," John interjected.

"Dougall, you are a freaking pacifist. Shut your pie

hole; let the real men take care of this."

John watched how McGee stood in the middle of the road waiting for the truck. He was insane. Everyone knew it, but no one dared to stand up to him.

The truck stopped, and a tall officer stepped out of the truck and saluted McGee. In perfect English, the German said that he was surrendering himself and his remaining men to the American Army. As Haas dropped his salute, McGee yelled at the Germans to dismount and line up.

"Hands *hoch*!"

All the Germans put their hands up.

"Now! Jeff!"

Jeffcoat fired in short bursts.

"*Auf den Boden,*" McGee laughed sarcastically.

The Germans dropped one by one. The Sergeant finished them with pistol shots. The last to die was the tall officer. When McGee had his .45 pointed at his forehead, the German stood up. This took McGee by surprise and he froze for a second; the officer looked him in the eyes in a last muted plea. McGee shot him in the chest and Haas lurched backwards and landed beside his men. The deed was done.

OLD DEMONS

"Only the winners decide what war crimes were."

GARY WILLS

Brant waited to see if there was more to the story. John leaned back in the chair and looked at the empty glass. Breathing heavily, the old man ended his confession with a raspy voice:

"Less than a week later our platoon got hit with artillery. McGee, Jeffcoat and others bought it. I got away without a scratch. Sometimes, I wonder why."

To watch his father's anguish was a burden almost beyond what Brant could handle. The whiskey warmed his throat as he looked at his dad, who seemed transported back in time. Brant couldn't believe that he was finally hearing the secret of the Journal. He pondered how much his mother knew about it. Just over four years ago, Margarie had asked Brant to confirm an address in Bamberg. She never told him the reason behind her request, but had instructed him to check if a Haas family still lived there.

He thought about Tanja and the first time they met. He had knocked on the door to ask in his broken German, "*Kennen Sie* Family Haas?"

Tanja spoke perfect English and said, "My mother's maiden name is Haas."

Their connection was instant and Brant stood there and stared at Tanja until the point of it being awkward. She smiled politely and broke the ice, "Are you going to stand there or are you going to actually say something?"

Brant looked at his feet and mumbled that he was sorry for staring; he was just trying to honor his mother's request to find the Haas family. Tanja invited Brant in and offered him a cup of coffee. She was curious as to why an American was searching for her family. Brant did not have a lot of details to offer except that his parents had met in Bamberg and that now his mother asked him to find the Haas family.

"She probably knows my mother or my grandmother,"

Tanja concluded.

A few weeks later, Brant found himself downtown with his battle buddy having an early beer in one of the basement bars known as a Keller. The bar was plastered with posters advertising Honey Bee and the T-Bones, a Rock-a-Billy group that seemed to draw a pretty good crowd. Brant and Chuck were sitting close to the stage as mostly Germans filled the club. By the time the band started playing, both senior non-commissioned officers were pretty well lubricated. He turned around and saw Tanja standing at the back of the room. She was trying to get closer to the stage, but the crowd was pretty packed. Knowing that he was almost too drunk to be in public, he asked Chuck to see if Tanja wanted to sit with them by the stage. Chuck went up to Tanja, and slowly they moved back together towards the front. As she sat down, he could feel that he was going to make a fool of himself. Luckily, Tanja could not hear most of the craziness he was spewing.

As the night went on, Tanja consumed enough alcohol to render Brant's antics tolerable. These included, but were not limited to, him threatening the bass player's life in order to convince the band to play a slow song in honor of Tanja, and ripping down the poster on the door as they were leaving to keep as a souvenir. Brant thought back to that night and wondered how in the world that led to him marrying her and having a beautiful baby girl. Tanja was now pregnant with their second child, and he couldn't imagine life without them. His failed first marriage nearly ended his career and stopped him from going to Officer Candidate School. Now that he was getting close to retirement, his marriage to Tanja was a blessing in ways he could not even put into words.

***

The fasten seatbelt sign chimed on and the pilot announced the current time and temperature at Frankfurt International Airport. John tensed in anticipation of the landing. He looked at Brant and wondered how the next week would change their lives and affect their family. Brant looked pale and uneasy himself. John cued into his son's nervousness, "Brant, please forgive me for sharing my burden with you."

"Dad, you never lost your honor. You and I need God's help for what we are about to experience."

As they made their way out of the terminal, a very pregnant Tanja waddled toward them. She was holding Sophia.

"*Willkommen Papa!*"

John looked at Tanja and then at Sophia and was overcome with emotion. Brant grabbed his dad's arm and held him up.

"Are you okay?"

John quickly shook Brant off and regained his composure.

"I'm alright…jet lag."

The drive from Frankfurt to Bamberg was about two hours. John sat in the back with Sophia and couldn't keep his eyes off of her. He could feel the love coming through the eyes of this little girl. She kept saying, "Opa, look," and "Opa, I am having a little brother," and "Opa, where is Oma?" Brant and Tanja had often spoken of the American grandparents, shown Sophia pictures of them, and insisted that John talk to her on the phone.

Although Margarie died before her granddaughter was born, little Sophia still seemed to know so much about her, and if he squinted his own eyes just a little, he could find the reflection of his dear wife in little Sophia's cheery face. He started telling her about Oma, and how beautiful she was, and that she had gone to heaven so that she could watch over everyone. As he told her of his faith in the simplest of terms, he realized that he truly believed it; that Margarie was indeed in heaven looking down on them all.

When he looked into Sophia's innocent eyes, John thought less of his burden. This beautiful angel was his grandchild and he wanted to enjoy her smile a bit longer. Haas could wait a few more days. Then, he would journey on to the spot where the Journal ended and his personal nightmare began. He would make things right and ... that would be it. He had only a little life left in him; finally he could see the end of his private battle.

Tanja was nervous and talked non-stop, going from English to German and then a combination of both. She was trying so hard to make John welcome.

"So, Tanja, Brant never told me how you two met."

Brant turned and almost drove off the road, drawing a reproachful glare from his wife.

"Well, Papa, Brant knocked on my door four years ago. He was looking for someone his mother knew; he was very nervous - and very cute, I might add. We talked for a bit, he said thanks, and left. I met him a couple of weeks later downtown, and we have been together ever since, except for when the Army takes him away from me."

***

Driving towards Bamberg had brought back so many memories. John was having a hard time processing how everything revolved around coming back to this town. It was meant to be... He knew he had to get things straight. All he knew was that it was a little town on the Rhine, and the pine grove at the intersection. He could see every detail. In an instant he was back in the pine groves, he could smell the pines, the dirt, and that distinct smell of blood.

"Dougall, when I come back in the morning, I want

there to be no sign of this. If I can find anything, I guarantee you that you will spend eternity with these Krauts... Since you love them so much you can make sure they get a 'proper burial.' Just to let you know, I don't really give a rat's ass if they are buried or not. I just know that leaving them out in the sun to bake is going to cause me problems. You know about my brother these Nazi's killed. I am serious Dougall. Leave no sign they ever existed."

McGee jumped into the jeep and sped away, leaving John with a shovel and an unspeakable mission. Just below the execution site was a crater from one of the many bombs that had been dropped. If he worked through the night, he could fill it in with the surrounding dirt and the German soldiers. It was slow, tedious work but finally he got the men laying together, two deep, four in a row. The last body he positioned was Haas's. Every time he looked at him, his open eyes, and the look on his face simply said...*why?* At daybreak the next morning, the Germans were buried, the ground was flat, and he stood at the crossroads looking at a pine grove that witnessed the evil he had just been party to. Around noon, Sergeant McGee returned and simply motioned for John to get back in the jeep.

That night, under a bright, full moon he labored to save his own life, knowing that if he didn't conceal this crime he would join the Germans. It was then that he promised to someday make it right; he would come back after the war, help recover the remains, and then confess the events so Sergeant McGee would be court-martialed. It never happened. He was never able to muster the courage to tell anyone what happened or to return.

***

As they turned into the US Army base, John felt he

was home. He enjoyed the crisp salute that the gate MPs snapped when they saw his military ID. Everything was freshly painted and polished. The car drove slowly as it passed a platoon marching in cadence. John almost joined in humming the song. *Yes... this is my world, and here is where I'll find the strength I need*, he thought, admiring the young soldiers going about their business.

The house was a standard military home like so many others on Warner Barracks. Tanja, like any good German homemaker, had pots of flowers everywhere. Brant jumped out of the car and started lifting out the bags. Tanja tended to Sophia as they walked into the house. John followed them into a spacious living room. When he saw the painting, he felt the shock.

It can't be, he thought.

Tanja caught his stare and offered, "Do you like it? It's an Imperial *Adler*...the eagle. My grandmother got it as a gift, many years after the war from someone in Hamburg."

At that very moment, Sophia ran to him and grabbed his leg.

"Opa, Opa, Opa! *Wasser, ich moechte Wasser...*"

＊＊＊

Brant took off early in the morning. He was busy getting ready for his next deployment; he had turned silent and seemed as overwhelmed as his father. Brant struggled to balance his job's duties with the need to be with John. He took heat from several directions. His chain of command was concerned that he had missed several key deployment related appointments.

Mike called out of the blue and wanted to come

"to help". Brant mustered his most diplomatic reply when he simply told his troubled brother that their father needed space to resolve what happened in his past.

"*Liebchen*, are you going to be ok?" Tanja looked at her husband with concern.

"Yeah, don't worry about a thing," Brant said reassuringly.

As a young, married couple they survived the last deployment with relative ease. Tanja had always been independent and Brant was older, more mature and had plenty of responsibilities to keep his mind off missing his wife. Tanja became pregnant with Sophia when he was on R and R leave midway in 2006. They had not planned the pregnancy, but when he heard the news, he was euphoric. Brant, the soldier who liked to plan everything with care, felt the surge of emotions in enjoying the unplanned.

Neither Tanja nor John knew that Brant was dealing with his own demons.

MORE DEMONS

"Death is a delightful hiding place for weary men."

HERODOTUS

Brant's former company commander had asked him to give the memorial eulogy for Specialist Kowalski. He had never clicked with her and now that Brant had stepped up to work as the battalion training non-commissioned officer, the relationship with the Captain had gone from bad to worse. It was obvious that the Captain thought the suicide would mar her career and she was interested in shifting the focus away from herself and onto Sergeant Dougall. Nonetheless, he had something to say about his soldier and he knew that it would be important for the rest of the platoon to bring some closure.

The commander made some brief remarks and mentioned that Sergeant First Class Dougall had been the platoon sergeant for 2nd Platoon. As Brant walked up to the podium he looked at Kowalski's boots, and the dog tags that hung from the grip of the rifle with his helmet perched on top of it. Technically, this was a remembrance ceremony, and not a memorial ceremony. Because the soldier had taken his own life there were some subtle differences. The display that memorialized him as a soldier was usually not used during a remembrance ceremony; however the Sergeant Major made the call that Specialist Kowalski would be remembered as a soldier who had served his country with honor.

Brant grabbed the sides of the lectern and in a strong voice started the Eulogy, "It is my honor and privilege to speak today about the life of Specialist Kowalski.

Exactly three years ago today, I arrived here in Germany and was assigned as the Platoon Sergeant for 2nd Platoon. The company was preparing for Iraq. As a new Platoon Sergeant, I understood very quickly that the soldiers of 2nd Platoon were special. Each and every one of them pulled their weight, did their duty, and ensured that our rotation was successful down range. Now we all share the loss of one of our brothers. Over the past few days, several people have asked me about Specialist George Kowalski. Who was he? I can describe him in one word: Warrior. George was a warrior, plain and simple. He strove to be the best possible gunner. He knew that a gunner's expertise could save lives. George and his marksmanship made us feel safe in some of the most adverse situations. George loved our platoon and he showed it every day through his actions. He always had time to listen and to help. You would be hard pressed to find someone in the company who hasn't been touched by George's humor and practical jokes, from mimicking the movie Team America to drinking straight from your coffee cup. Words fail to convey what a tremendous loss we are all experiencing, but I do know that we all are better for having known Specialist George Kowalski. A Sermon written by Canon Scott Holland has given me comfort and I feel that this is a message George would want us to hear:

Death is nothing at all. It does not count. I have only slipped away into the next room. Nothing has happened. Everything remains exactly as it was. I am I, and you are you, and the old life that we lived so fondly together is untouched, unchanged. Whatever we were to each other, that we are still. Call me by the old familiar name. Speak of me in the easy way which you always used. Put no difference into your tone. Wear no forced air of sorrow. Laugh as we always laughed at the little jokes that we enjoyed together. Play, smile, think of me, and pray for me. Let my name be ever the household word that it always was. Let it be spoken without an effort, without the ghost of a shadow upon it. Life means all that it ever meant. It is the same as it ever was. There is absolute and unbroken continuity. Why should I be out of mind because I am out of sight? I am but waiting for you, for an interval, somewhere very near, just around the corner. All is well. Nothing is hurt; nothing is lost. One brief moment and all will be as it was before. How we shall laugh at the trouble of parting when we meet again!

Brant looked over at the picture of George.

"George felt responsible for the lives of fellow soldiers, but also for the lives of the civilians caught in the merciless gears of war. His noble mind had its troubles coping with events he could not control…"

Fighting off a shiver Brant closed with, "George, we love you, and we miss you. Rest in peace, brother."

***

The last rotation had been brutal and Brant had made choices that he was having a hard time coming to terms with. As Platoon Sergeant, he had been riding with one of his squads. As they maneuvered the streets of Mosul, he saw the lead truck clear an intersection. A small, orange car sped towards the convoy. The recent string of suicide vehicle borne improvised explosive devices or SVBIEDS had taken its toll on soldiers in Mosul. The lead gunner turned, picked up his alternate weapon, an M249, and fired into the vehicle. The vehicle crossed in front of the convoy and came to rest about fifty feet from the intersection. Brant grabbed the medic and went towards the vehicle.

That's when a large crowd gathered around the vehicle and pulled its driver out. The driver held his stomach as blood ran into the street.

"Doc, see what you can do…"

With that direction, the Doc opened up the driver's shirt, revealing an abdominal wound with parts of his intestine coming out. Brant had to make a decision; the crowd was getting larger and Doc was starting to freak out.

"Sergeant, what do we do? They are surrounding us."

"What can you do for his wound?"

"Not much. I can put an abdominal bandage around him, but he has to get to a trauma center now."

Brant decided that since they had shot him, they would transport him to the American Combat Support Hospital. Doc and Brant loaded the driver into the HUMMV. The old man was pretty light and sat upright holding his stomach, screaming in pain. Brant got on the radio and called in a casualty evacuation. He communicated that the injury was urgent surgical and was asked for the specifics.

"Doc, tell me what I need to tell them."

"Sergeant, he has an eviscerated intestine."

"What the hell? Give me something I can say."

"Sergeant, tell them his guts are hanging out."

As Brant turned to the driver, the old man looked at him and said... *Mai, Mai!* Brant knew not to give water to a man with a stomach injury. He looked him in the eye and said no.

As the convoy pulled up to the hospital, a crew came out with a stretcher and whisked the Iraqi into the triage room. Brant walked into the hospital and came face to face with a nurse he had seen the previous week when he was suffering from "Saddam's Revenge," a severe intestinal sickness that fully earned its name. The nurse asked Brant how he was feeling and smiled. Brant held up his bloodied hands and asked if he could wash them.

"So, is this a good guy or bad guy?" the nurse said, in what could be construed as a flirtatious tone. Brant thought about the question and realized that the true answer was that he was just a guy in the wrong place at the wrong time. He could see the staff stripping off the man's clothes. The wound was fully exposed. The doctor came over to Brant,

"You have any questions, son?"

"Just one, Sir. Is he going to live?"

"Yes, for about four hours."

Brant could not believe the lack of emotion in the doctor's tone. He caught the old man's eyes, the terror, and then the gurney was slowly rolled away.

"Sir, what do you need from me?"

"Nothing. You're good. Be safe out there." And with that it was done. Brant felt like he had just dropped off a piece of lost luggage.

He walked outside and the vehicles were lined up, all eyes were on him. About that time the company commander came out and he could see that the conversation was not going to go well.

"Sergeant Dougall, is that man going to live?"

"No, Ma'am he is not"…Brant slowly leaned over to the commander and whispered, "Ma'am, be very careful what you do and say in the next few minutes. That gunner did his job, and if you aren't careful you are going to send the wrong message to these soldiers and you will get someone killed."

The commander glared at Sergeant Dougall and asked him, "What's your gunner's name?"

"Specialist Kowalski, Ma'am."

"I will speak to you later Sergeant. Finish your mission."

Later that night, in the tactical operations center, the Sergeant Major approached Brant, "I talked with your commander, Dougall. She does understand the situation… We have rules of engagement to help us stay on the right side. Your gunner made the call in a split second, under intense stress, and fear of imminent death; to judge such a man you need the context to measure his actions against some rules, you need empathy. Put yourself in his shoes in that very instant before you cast a stone. That holds true when you judge yourself too. There is no doubt in my mind that you and your gunner both acted correctly."

That short chat helped Brant. Nevertheless, when the deaths and the stress piled up, he started to have nightmares. He became edgy and moody and at times, completely disconnected.

Just like my dad, he thought.

SIBERIA

"It requires more courage to suffer than to die."
NAPOLEON BONAPARTE

Carla Haas pressed her face against the walls of the boxcar. The cool draft seeping through the plank boards diluted the stench of death, unwashed bodies and human waste. She had a terrible migraine caused by dehydration. The bucket for drinking water standing next to the sliding door had been empty for two days. No one knew when it might be filled again. The train kept moving eastward through endless forests carrying dying, human wrecks that only two weeks ago were German soldiers captured in Crimea.

***

The front collapsed too fast for standard evacuation plans to be effective. Soviet tanks and self-propelled guns, followed by infantry blocked all the hospital exits and trapped all the wounded and the medical staff. A short, merciless triage had the staff and ambulatory wounded corralled into a staging area. The remaining Germans were executed in their hospital beds.

A short and wiry NKVD Captain interrogated Carla. As soon as it became apparent that she did not have any valuable information, he sent her with another group of German nurses to the railroad platform. On the way, the Russians from the escort detail pulled them onto the side of the road and started to rape them. One younger woman jumped over the fence and tried to run. The guards did not bother to follow her. One of them dropped to his knee and aimed his rifle. One shot. The running woman fell down. Carla watched in shock and disbelief as two Russian soldiers approached her with lusty looks. She decided to live.

Nobody raped them during the train trip. Carla believed that the train commander was very strict and his soldiers had more discipline than the NKVD guards. The cynical thought that crossed her mind was that the prisoners became too filthy and unappealing for their guards.

***

When the train finally stopped at the POW labor camp, and the doors slid open, light flooded the insides of the cattle boxcar. Several bodies were piled in the middle, and the survivors were almost delirious. For them a new triage process began. Because of their medical background, most of the nurses ended up in a 'special hospital' for POWs. Here Carla met Sidorov, an older Russian officer in charge of camp security. Colonel Pavel Sidorov's daughter died during the German siege of Leningrad, only one of the countless tragedies that ravaged the lives of the Russian people during the war. The daughter's loss turned Sidorov to the forbidden spirituality of the Russian Orthodoxy, the centuries old faith still undefeated by Communism. The staff and the prisoners had little inkling that behind the appearance of a draconian disciplinarian, the *Comrade Colonel* brimmed with compassion.

When Carla's pregnancy became noticeable, everybody assumed it to be the consequence of an unreported rape. Carla knew better but kept silent and carried on with her duties as before. On the day one of the guards ordered her to report to the security compound, Carla feared the worst.

"…Carla Haas?"

"Yes, Comrade Colonel."

Sidorov studied her with his piercing blue eyes. His bushy eyebrows did little to ease the coldness of his gaze and Carla felt a drop of sweat on her forehead despite the biting cold.

"… How many months?"

"Four… I am sorry… five months, Comrade."

"Prisoner, your condition qualifies you for a special camp for mothers with children. Those are better equipped to accommodate this type of case."

Carla started crying, fearing that any change could bring more pain and uncertainty. Sidorov came around his desk and placed a white handkerchief in her hands. On impulse Carla fell to her knees begging for help. The Colonel kept quiet. Carla stood up and struggled to regain composure knowing that her tears could trigger ridicule, even reprisal.

"Do you know I had a daughter just like you…young and beautiful? She died of hunger in Leningrad."

Carla froze. What can a German expect from this grieving father? Hate and nothing more… She was instantly heart sick. She waited in silence for the guard to take her back to the medical huts.

Sidorov called her to his office again two days later with an unexpected and intriguing proposition. His wife had a medical condition that required the presence of a nurse twenty-four hours a day. Carla would come and live in their home and she could remain there after her child was born. Carla accepted with both hope and apprehension. It was the best decision of her life.

The only medical condition that Carla could attribute to Mrs. Sidorova was "healthy as an ox." For the next couple of years, Carla and her daughter Nadia lived buffered from the harshness and brutality of the POW camp. Carla became proficient in Russian while Nadia spoke it like a native. Both called Mrs. Sidorova "babushka."

***

Red star, painted trucks puffed grey exhaust as they passed through Hermannnstadt's downtown. Grim looking Russian soldiers followed them on foot in long columns. When the Romanians changed sides, the whole of the Balkans crumbled like a house of cards. The once undefeated Germans, abandoned Greece and Yugoslavia and hastened to shorten their front.

Rudolf's grandfather watched the Soviets pouring through the city with uncharacteristically open concern. Hard times are coming, he thought. With a tinge of sadness, he reflected that Siebenburger Saxons' era was coming to an end. He heard rumors. Young Germans started to be summoned by the new conquerors and deported to the USSR as forced labor. Old age spared Rudolf's grandparents that fate. They lived as before in their roomy house enjoying their large garden and a small orchard in the back. The old man's savings and his small, watch repair shop afforded them enough money to live comfortably. They lost contact with Rudolf and Carla, but they managed to keep a tenuous correspondence with their daughter—Rudolf's mother.

In 1947, in the face of rampant inflation, Soviet advisors had nudged the Romanian government to reform their currency. The banks had exchanged only a limited amount of money, effectively wiping out most of the old man's savings overnight. Stricken with grief, he fell ill. He passed away in his bed worrying about his wife, missing his daughter and his grandson. His wife followed him in '48.

***

Once the war ended, high hopes gripped the POW population. However, the years passed by and the hopes died with the detainees. Poor diet, overwork, disease and deadly winters thinned the ranks of the Axis soldiers interned in the Russian Gulag. For Carla, the plight of her former colleagues brought on intense feelings of guilt. She wrote tens of letters addressed to Rudolf's house in Bamberg that she passed to Sidorov. She did not know at that time that the Colonel never sent them. Sidorov was too canny to risk having one of them intercepted by the NKVD. He kept all of them in a safe inside his house.

In 1948, the Soviets released some of the East European POWs. Carla approached Sidorov and asked him to look into the new opportunity as she could claim Polish ancestry. Sidorov could not make any promises. Carla was a former nurse in a German military hospital, and she had only German papers. He did, however, pursue the matter. After six months, the official answer came that Carla Haas could not claim Polish citizenship, and that she did not meet the requirements for release. Carla asked him to appeal the decision.

Sidorov told her gently, "My predecessor killed himself. He shot himself in the head... twice. Hard head I guess... Anyway, the point is you should try to be as anonymous as possible here in our proletarian heaven. If you swim against the current, you'll disappear. If a person has past accomplishments, then they may get the honor of a poorly disguised suicide."

Just like the Nazis, thought Carla.

Pavel Sidorov died in the winter of 1951. Carla's world came crashing down on her. She was forced to leave the refuge that allowed her to raise her daughter in relative safety and return to a POW special camp. Nadia suffered the most as she got pneumonia almost immediately. The meager food consisted mainly of boiled buckwheat and potato soup with lard. Poor hygiene and bitter cold made recovery from sickness a very iffy affair. Carla saved every bit of food she could spare as well as some chunks of sugar, the rarest of all treats for Nadia. Mrs. Sidorova brought them some antibiotics and that saved the child's life.

Babushka pulled Carla aside and told her, "Pavel did not send your letters. I found them in one of his locked drawers. I will mail them when I return to Leningrad. I cannot stay here any longer. I will try to contact some of Pavel's friends to see if I can get you out with me. You are the only family I have left."

Carla's eyes became misty.

"Babushka, you and your husband were my angels. I've given up hope for myself but please take Nadia with you. Help her have a normal life."

Mrs. Sidorova could not take Nadia, so she decided to extend her stay as long as she could. For Carla and Nadia, her visits and her kindness represented the anchor of their lives.

In 1954, Stalin did the world a favor and expired. Conditions in the camp improved slightly. Finally, in 1955, Carla and Nadia joined the first batch of POWs set for release. They needed a whole month to cross the border into East Germany. In Berlin's *Bahnhof*, Carla entered a normal restroom for the first time in years. She turned on all the faucets and washed her hands with soap furiously. When she caught site of herself, she stopped, and looked deeply into the large mirror. She started shaking, ignoring the other women. The stranger looking back at her from the mirror had white hair framing her face and a fine web of crow's feet at the corners of her eyes. Nobody could have guessed that Carla was barely thirty-five years old and that Nadia was her daughter.

Carla started her search for Rudolf immediately. With a little luck she found Hans Beck, now a car mechanic in the *Weberwiese* neighborhood. Together they traced Rudolf's unit's movements in the last days of the war. Everything pointed to a West German town in the Ruhr region. Even though East Germany did not allow regular border crossings into the "rotten capitalist" side of Germany, Carla determined to get there anyway. Beck declared that he would arrange it.

***

Carla, Nadia and Beck escaped to West Berlin through the U-Bahn tunnel. Carla joked that the only preparation Beck did was to buy U-Bahn tickets. Beck answered with a smirk, "Rudi taught me that the most simple and direct plans are often the best."

"Thank you, Hans. I am fortunate to have a friend like you."

Carla moved in with Rudolf's mother in Bamberg. She spent many hours in Rudolf's room looking at photographs and crying. Her hopes faded away when she discovered his status listed as missing in every military record. Something was amiss. The few members of Haas's last unit that she contacted all confirmed that Rudolf had surrendered to the Americans in April 1945. There was no record of him on any POW list.

For Rudolf's mother, the joy of meeting Rudolf's wife and daughter at last was bitter-sweet. After years of dead-end quests, she begged Carla to abandon her search for Rudolf.

"Rudolf gave me you and Nadia. For this I am so grateful. Try to live your life looking ahead, not in the past. I despaired when I saw that no matter how hard I tried, I could not find my son. I know in my heart that he is dead and his grave is forgotten and unmarked. I did not leave a stone unturned. Rudolf is dead, my child."

THE SEARCH

"And into endless nothing I go, and leave no trace."

M. EMINESCU

Carla Haas did not give up her search for Rudolf. With help from veterans' organizations, she managed to track down several former members of 9th Panzer. Most of them had known Rudolf well. Their stories varied slightly but the common thread was the same: Rudolf's battalion had made its last stand in Siegburg and all the fighting had ceased on April 13th. One of the veterans, a former personnel clerk, gave Carla a roster of names of men from Haas's company.

"*Frau* Haas, this list predated the battle at Remagen. A lot of them are dead. However, if you find the survivors, they are the most likely to know what happened to your husband. *Viel Glueck!*"

Carla appealed to the German Police to find the addresses. They turned her down, invoking a litany of laws and internal rules and regulations. Carla did not give up. She insisted. Finally, in the good tradition of German authorities, she received a lengthy document that could be summed up with one word, "No!" She ratcheted up the pressure by threatening to go to a newspaper and pub-lish an article entitled: "Police Red Tape and Bureaucracy Drives Gulag Survivor to Suicide." For her effort, she got a psychiatric evaluation with a police escort, and a visit from a city official who quickly offered to check all the names on the roster.

After what felt like an eternity she got an address. When the reply to her initial inquiry via telegram came back, she boarded the train to Hamburg, filled with angst and hope. In her mind, she milled the prepared questions over and over, put them on a piece of paper, and then she became conscious that she knew them by heart. She tore the paper and tried to contain her impatience and calm her nervousness. She kept pulling at her above-the-knee skirt and picking imaginary lint from her very formal clothing. Nadia had told her when she left, "Mommy, you're dressed like our school principal."

Carla was not sure whether to take that as a compliment.

***

She spent hours looking out the windows at a landscape dotted with forests and cities bustling with construction sites. The reconstruction of Germany seemed unstoppable, with thousands of cranes actively erecting a concrete jungle at a fast pace. Carla shared her train compartment with a family of five led by a mustachioed, muscular man. The man and his wife had three children. Each was shy and quiet as they looked with curiosity at Carla. She offered them some chocolate. They hesitated, and then looked at their father who nodded. They ate it fast, licking their fingers, while the man said in a broken German, "*Danke, Fraulein.* I am Yusuf and this is my family. We came from Turkey. My brother found me a good job in Hamburg ...*viel Geld.*"

The man grinned, showing a row of tobacco-stained teeth. Carla smiled politely. She thought about Rudolf and his good-natured curiosity towards anything foreign, new and exotic. *Rudi would have made friends with them in a heartbeat.* Carla imagined Rudolf talking and joking with the Turks and a shadow of sadness came over her face. Yusuf's wife raised a small packet towards Carla and modestly offered her some dried fruit. It tasted good.

The train conductor announced Hamburg, and the Turks hurriedly grabbed their enormous luggage and headed towards the exit. Carla tried unsuccessfully to explain that Hamburg was the final destination and they would have plenty of time. Yusuf would not be persuaded by those arguments; he was on a mission to get off the train as soon as possible with his family. He barely had time to say goodbye over his shoulder.

***

Gunter Zelman had what might be called a small dwelling close to the docks. He graciously invited Carla in and offered her refreshments. The apartment had plenty of oil paintings, some only half-finished, and Carla struggled to warm their connection by complementing her host on his artistic prowess.

"Oh, it is just a hobby; I must paint houses to pay my bills," Zelman replied with false humility. "But I did one work for your husband… I painted an eagle on our Panther."

He started to dig through a stack of photos and produced one showing a young, wiry soldier straddled over a tank's main gun. On the tank's hull, Carla made out the faded contours of a black and white eagle with outspread wings.

"It was blue in reality and *Herr Hauptmann* loved it," Zelman pronounced with a hint of pride. "I have it on canvass too… Now; I want you to have it."

"Are you in this photo?" Carla asked trying to control her trembling voice.

"Yes!… I was very fit and slim then, not like now."

Carla glanced at Zelman and did not recognize the pear-shaped man in the skinny youngster in the picture.

"I could not keep myself in shape after my back injury," Zelman added, mostly in defense of his pride. "But I assume you'd want to see a picture with your husband."

Carla's pulse quickened. In her mind's eye she could see him perfectly. Did she want to risk replacing that perfect image with a grainy photo?

My Captain had great taste in women, thought Zelman

while pulling a framed photo from the drawer.

"I enlarged it and framed it for you *Frau* Haas."

Carla's eyes filled with tears. Rudolf looked tired and stressed but even in that aged photo his eyes had that boyish hopeful look that had swept her off her feet in the Crimea. She could barely hear Zelman talking away, clearly glad that he had the opportunity to share some memories:

"…We all liked him a lot. He really understood more about the war than anybody else I knew. I remember one night in January of '45, when I was on guard duty outside our command post. Rudi Haas and another Captain, Weiss, got their hands on some captured French cognac. It took them all of an hour to get really intoxicated, with Weiss sliding under the table in the process. Our Captain stumbled outside to relieve himself. Then he saw me. I snapped to attention; he smiled and asked me, "Do you trust our *Fuehrer*?"

"Yes, of course…Sir."

"Are you dumb, Gunter? That man is a fruit-cake!"

I started to shake like a leaf.

"Bitte, Hauptmann… please go to bed, you drank a bit too much."

Haas waved at me to shut my mouth and continued, "I have seen the young and old swept away by this madness. Even my father, whom I never expected to be thrilled by politics, could not resist Hitler's charisma. The Chancellor talked us into such uncensored frenzy, that he got away with everything. It is ironic that when we need a level-headed, rational leader to save what's left of the Fatherland, we get this fanatic to bury us all instead. We are all guilty for believing that we were fighting for a just cause. We are all guilty in this mess, and the retribution is coming…"

I froze terrified. Haas laughed and patted my shoulder, "I'll make sure you will not go down with the Nazis. You're a good kid."

I never forgot his words. It was surreal. The Captain never again opened up, but I knew he spoke his heart that evening."

"Herr Zelman, thank you for everything, but you probably know that what I need to hear from you is the truth of what happened to Rudolf."

Zelman sighed and sat down.

"Frau Haas, I was your husband's gunner... I can tell you that I never met a better man but it pains me to tell you that I really do not know what in fact happened to him. Last time I saw him, he was driving with another Captain towards the American lines. Later that day, we were all rounded up and sent to a POW camp but I did not see your husband among us. We assumed that they kept him in a separate camp or they used him as a translator of some sort because of his language skills."

"I know he is dead, Herr Zelman. I am not delusional. I just want to find his grave and put his name on a stone, say a prayer and show his daughter the final resting place of her father."

"I am so very sorry, Frau Haas. Many soldiers disappeared during those crazy days. There were mines everywhere, trigger happy pilots, even friendly fire from some die-hard Nazis. You may never find out what happened to him."

***

Back home, Carla phoned Hans Beck and told him that the key to her quest may be hidden somewhere in the German military archives. Haas crossed a lot of paths, and he never did anything without a plan or purpose. She felt him trying to connect with her in so many ways. Her Rudi would get his message to her; she just had to find out where he sent it. This was not over, there were answers and she would find them at any cost.

HANS BECK'S SECRET

"If the facts don't fit the theory, change the facts."

ALBERT EINSTEIN

No one knew the secret that Hans Beck carried for ten years, but Hans Beck. So he thought.

In 1933, as the Nazis started to ramp up their anti-Jewish rants, Beck was an unemployed, nineteen-year-old orphan. As soon as he landed a construction job, he started a one man quest to find his biological father. His mother had died during the big influenza pandemic of 1918, and she had always told Beck that his father was a sailor in the German Imperial Navy, who was captured in the Pacific by the British. At the war's conclusion, however, Beck's father never turned up to reclaim his son, so Hans ended up in an orphanage.

His quest to find his roots led Beck to his mother's birth place in Salzburg. When he decided to go and inquire of some distant relatives, they served him the same story; that his mother had him outside of wedlock with some sailor. Hans did not give up. He found in his mother's letters the address of a Swiss woman from Geneva. Beck deduced from the letter's tone, that his mother and the Swiss woman were close friends. She finally told Beck the truth.

"Your father was an Italian Jew, who had a one night stand with your mother. He never knew about you and your mother did not try to tell him either."

"Where is he now? Do you know?" asked a very skeptical Beck.

"Last I heard he went to Spain to fight for the Republicans. Some say he died there. But I do not know for sure."

"Do you have a picture?"

"Yes I do. He was our science teacher in high school. I do not know how he managed to sleep with your mother. He probably dazzled her with his intelligence. Very bright and very ugly ..."

A look at the sepia photo was enough for Beck. Same

chin and ears; there he was unmistakably, the "mysterious high seas hero", a teen seducer and a Jew! Beck decided that the "official story" of the unknown sailor was safer and stuck with it throughout the war.

***

On the eve of the Kursk battle, their company bivouacked on the banks of a shallow creek. At noon, the shallow river was full of young German soldiers doing what soldiers of all ages do when unoccupied - horse play. Stepping gingerly on his toes along the rocky ground and wearing some worn out underwear, Beck walked upstream alone and away from the commotion.

"Hans are you going to take a bath?"

Beck turned around to face Haas.

"Maybe Rudi, but I am not joining that homosexual party!"

"Come on Hans, I am pretty sure that your boxers will turn them all off."

That evening, a Captain wearing the dreaded SD sleeve insignia of the *Sicherheitsdienst*–the SS security, approached Beck.

How the hell did they find out? A sense of dread washed over Beck.

"Sergeant, I want to apologize for investigating you… we needed to follow up all these ridiculous anonymous accusations. I found the letter and I talked with your commander. Please let me congratulate you for the heroism with which your father honored Germany."

Beck's jaw dropped.

"My father… Sir…?"

"Rudi Haas told me everything. Sometimes, well-intentioned or overzealous people believe untrue rumors. I will put to rest those wild and false accusations. Good luck tomorrow. Heil Hitler!"

The meeting left Beck seriously unnerved and with butterflies in his stomach. He hurried up to Haas's tent.

"Rudi!!!" he whispered.

"Come in Hans!"

Before he opened his mouth, Haas handed him an envelope.

"I always wondered why you act like an enthusiastic Nazi. You better memorize this and stick with this story from now on. This is a letter that your father's captors wrote to your mother."

The envelope contained a letter dated 1914 and in English. Beck looked bewildered at Haas. "Are you in the forgery business now Rudi?"

"Your father was a sailor on the SMS Emden. An Australian cruiser sunk Emden and captured the surviving crew. Your father died of wounds, and the nice Australian Captain wrote a letter to your mother."

"Rudi, how long did it take you to come up with this, and how did you fool that SS officer?"

"He is a pompous moron, so I served him a pompous story."

"He did not look moronic to me; he's an SD investigator for the love of God…"

"Ok, you have a point… he is a scary moron."

Beck tried to smile without much success. He was still shaken.

"Hans… when some deranged, Jew-hunting zealot is threatening to take away my best platoon leader I can be very creative. Please do not think about that anymore, and get some sleep… Tomorrow someone else is going to hunt you… the Bolsheviks."

***

Haas tried hard to get Beck transferred with him when he left for France. It was impossible. Beck remained on the Russian front until the end. He witnessed one disaster after another as the Red Army delivered crippling blows to the dwindling German war machine. One of the more unsettling experiences was witnessing the incredible Russian strength. It seemed that the communist hordes could punch holes in the thin German defenses with impunity. Nothing could stop the red deluge. Beck gave up hope of outliving that inferno.

During the final battle for Berlin, every sane German soldier saw the writing on the wall. Their battalion had been reduced to a platoon-sized force without any fuel for their remaining Tigers. By that time, their outfit was a mix of *Wehrmacht* and SS with paramilitary replacements - a ragtag of infantry and tankers backed by *Hitlerjugend* and *Volkssturm*.

The commander, desperate to save the lives of his men, decided to surrender. He waved a white bed sheet and walked towards a Soviet tank. When the Russian tank commander opened the hatch and raised himself up, an SS sniper shot him in the face. The Soviet fell inside the turret leaving a fine red mist in the air. Both sides paused for a second trying to understand what had just happened. The German officer caught in the open disappeared in a cloud of smoke and dust as the Russians opened up on him with everything they had. Beck had never seen a body reduced to atoms before. His preservation instinct kicked in.

"My tankers will try to get on top of that building," he roared and sprinted into an adjacent alley followed closely by his men. They changed direction several times keeping piles of rubble between them and the Russians. Breathing heavily, Beck whispered his final order, "This war is over. Everyone get out of here and try to stay alive!"

After his comrades got away, Beck found refuge in a

basement full of dead civilians. He threw away his uniform and swapped it with civilian clothes he removed from the corpses. He spent several days in hiding, pretending to be dead until the gunfire died out. When he got out, bearded and dusty, he had difficulty keeping his eyes open. Blinking hard, he approached a Russian checkpoint.

"*Pozhaluĭsta, hleb,*" he uttered with a weak voice.

The Russians threw him the piece of black, dried bread he had called out for. Beck started to eat it fast, looking around to orientate himself. He saw how the Russians checked all the males for the SS underarm tattoo. He started to remove his shirt, when the Russians started to laugh.

"*Nyet, nyet* old man...you can pass..."

"Being short and fat is a blessing sometimes... but old... for God's sake, how can this be, I'm only 31," reflected a philosophical Beck.

* * *

After his uneventful escape across the Iron Curtain, Hans Beck opened his own import-export business. In less than three years, his tenacity and the rapid growth of the West German economy made him a rich man. He visited Carla often, spoiling Nadia with presents and sweets and making sure that Rudi's family felt no financial hardships. Because Carla did not accept his money he found creative ways to help. He remodeled her entire house because he wanted "to preserve a historical gem," and invested in a private clinic that, soon after, offered Carla the head nurse position.

She called him, grateful, "Thank you, my dear friend... I do not know how to repay you for all your kindness and help."

"Nonsense… I still owe Rudi much more."

In 1957, Beck sponsored a post-graduate history student to write a thesis on the last days of 9th Panzer Division and told him to dig up any documents referring to German prisoners. The student got his PhD and Beck got a very revealing photocopy from the German war archives.

On a cold and rainy, November evening, Hans Beck knocked on Carla's door. Nadia opened the door and hugged him.

"Mom, Uncle Hans is here!!"

Carla came and took his wet coat.

"Come in and get warm, Hans. I know how much you hate the cold."

"I have something for you, Carla."

"Hans, please stop! You do not owe us anything and we are doing quite well now. I make more than enough money and I can't accept help from you anymore. There are a lot of people out there who would be happy to benefit from your generosity, I am sure."

Hans sighed. He stared at the fireplace and avoided Carla's eyes. Finally, he stood up, took out an envelope, and passed it to Carla Haas. When he spoke, he sounded like an old man, "This time is different. I am very sorry."

Carla stared at him in disbelief. She opened the paper and asked, "English?"

"The translation is on the back."

"There are no names, Hans."

"Everything matches, Carla. Look at the date, the location, see here: two German officers in black uniform. That means they were tankers. This is not a coincidence. And there is a name: Dougall."

Carla covered her eyes and whispered, "I knew this in my heart, Hans."

"Well, this makes it official, I suppose. And it should

bring you some peace at last."

* * *

Hans Beck moved to Spain. He pursued his search for his father but instead found a soul mate. Carla received a last letter with photos from him in 1975, from Barcelona. In one picture, a smiling Beck was holding hands with a middle-aged woman with curly hair. Both looked happy.

THE CRIME SCENE

"Dishonored let me perish, an outcast among men."

M. EMINESCU

"Dad, we need to talk."

John sensed the seriousness in Brant's voice.

"Son, what's up?"

"What are your plans …with the Journal?"

"Well, I need to find an address and," John paused awkwardly to clear his throat, adding a quieter, "and then we'll see from there."

"You need to find an address or a person?"

"I don't know Brant, I need to find his family."

"I think you only need to find Haas's grave."

"That too, Son… but before that, I need to be come clean and tell his surviving family members, if any, what a piece of work I am."

"They know, Dad."

John's stomach muscles cramped.

"What are you talking about?"

"Dad, can't you see it? It is all too clear. The last thing I wanted to do was to cause you more pain. You know Mom just wanted me to find the family so she could help you do what you are doing now. I never told her that I did find the family. After meeting Tanja, I just blocked out the reality of the situation. I didn't know about Captain Haas or the details of the Journal. I just knew that I had met someone that loved me for me, and looked at me the way Mom looked at you. This is bigger than us, and I don't know what it means, but it feels like we are being given a second chance. Then there is Sophia; she is the blessing of this tragedy."

***

Brant could feel his father's pain; he couldn't imagine meeting the family of the old man that his own gunner killed. He knew that it was just the environment and his gunner had done what he was trained to do. There had been an investigation and the outcome was exactly that; considering the intelligence about suicide bombers and the actions of the driver - the shooting was justified.

No investigation had cleared his father's conscience. Over the past sixty years, he had tortured himself and self-medicated. Now, it was time to bring it to an end, for better or for worse.

***

"Brant, will you go with me? I just want it to be you and me with the German Police."

"Sure, Dad."

John couldn't fathom why the Haas family wasn't furious with him and he was prepared for them to turn on him once they saw the true horror at the gravesite. Brant agreed and they started the journey to link up with the local Polizei. It was less than two hours drive. When they got close to the place, it became evident that their journey had taken a turn into pure theatrics.

News trucks and a crowd waited for them as they entered the town. Polizei swarmed around the vehicle and the doors opened.

"Herr Dougall, Willkommen to Siegburg. I am sorry for the media; we must have had some leaks... We have found the place with the intersection and the pine grove and our agents are already digging. I can escort you there and we can get rid of the press."

The pictures snapped and the microphones were everywhere.

"Herr Dougall, is it true that you executed German soldiers? Herr Dougall, do you think you should be tried as a war criminal? Herr Dougall, are you here to confess?"

This is what John had expected. As he looked at the crowd, he could feel the hatred. It is what he felt about himself over the years. This confirmed that what he was doing was right.

"*Hallo, Ich bin Polizeirat Gerhauser*...sorry, I am Captain Gerhauser of the German Criminal Police, thank you for contacting us. It is very important for us to recover the war dead, and I understand that you also want to bring this matter to an end."

As they walked to the intersection, he saw more than thirty men digging in the exact spot he had described over the phone to the Captain.

"We have a machine that we use to locate the remains. It is basically a sort of radar, and we roll it over the ground and can see different shapes. We have discovered what appear to be four sets of remains."

John realized that he had not told the Germans that there were eight bodies. It didn't matter now. In less than an hour the whole grisly truth would be revealed.

* * *

As the German Polizei recovered the remains, John just sat and watched, recognizing the order in which they were recovered. At the end of the day, the skeletons lay in the sun. He walked over to them and saw the mud-caked bones wrapped in rotten wool. He walked straight to Haas and knelt down; he looked at his hand and saw the wedding ring. How could he ever make this right? This man could have been saved if he had found the courage to stand up for what was right. Then, the image of Sophia blinded him... knowing that he would have been killed by McGee. He sat there weeping uncontrollably. Brant walked up to his father.

"Dad, try to keep it together. These men were fighting for their country, just as you were. I know that you hold yourself responsible for his death, but I have a vote in this. You tortured yourself over something you couldn't control. It is time to move on, let the dead take care of the dead. Dad, my platoon was responsible for killing an innocent man, only now do I understand that it wasn't my call. We have to let it go… We have to focus on the living."

John turned to Brant; he could see himself so clearly. It was like looking in a mirror and he was speaking to himself, giving forgiveness. He felt weak, his heart was beating so fast he felt it was about to explode. He asked again for Brant to forgive him.

"Dad, it is not my place to forgive you… that is between you and God. You have been a great father to me, and I just want you to enjoy your grandchildren. This is not an end, this is a beginning."

***

It was quiet. John could hear a constant beep and he felt held close and safe, like he was swaddled. He could not explain it, but it must surely be the end. John opened his eyes. He saw that he was no longer at the gravesite, but tucked into clean, white sheets, lying under bright lights and with everyone staring down at him. He was in a hospital.

***

Mike got off the phone with Brant and sunk to his knees, he knew that his father was not coming back. Mike looked around his dingy apartment, there was barely any furniture and it reeked of cigarette and pot smoke. Most of his stuff was at the pawn shop and he barely made it from paycheck to paycheck. His addictions, laziness and contempt for authority had locked him into a seemingly unbreakable cycle. So many chances - college, job opportunities and even simple kindnesses from friends of his parents and he had blown them all. He had even taken great joy, on occasion, when he really embarrassed his family. Mike considered them do-gooders and when he could make a score off of them, whether it was money or something he could pawn, it was with a great sense of accomplishment. The only thing he could do is call his oldest brother and ask him to help him get to Germany before his father died.

"Hey John, this is Mike."

"What in the hell do you want, Mike? No, let me guess, just a hundred dollars to hold you over because someone screwed you on something. I thought I told you never to call me again, and yes I know that Dad is in the hospital. I just got off the phone with Brant, and no, I am not rushing to his side. We have said our goodbyes and he is finishing whatever the hell he needed to finish over there."

"John, I just want to see him before he goes. I'll get the money back to you. I promise."

"Mike, let me be very clear with you. No! Just out of curiosity, I added up how much you are into me, including the car that you are driving around in - ten thousand bucks. You have nickel and dimed me for too long. I wouldn't mind if you actually would get on your feet but all you care about is getting your next fix and then sticking it to someone - goodbye!"

As the phone clicked off, Mike was more alone than he had ever felt before. Then it hit him. He would call on Pastor Thomas; after all the time they spent in the church there is no way he would say no. Mike jumped in the car and sped to the church. It was Wednesday and he knew he could find the pastor in his office. Over the years his parents had spent so much time in the church that he knew the movements of everyone in that building, and Wednesday was an open office day for the pastor. As he rushed into the church office the secretary caught him.

"Mike, what are you doing and what is wrong?"

"It's my dad. He is getting ready to die and I need to get to him."

About that time, the pastor came out of the office and just shook his head.

"Get in here, Mike."

The pastor listened intently to Mike's plea and request for enough money to get to Germany.

"Mike, this is going to be painful for you to hear. You going to Germany is only for you to comfort yourself. Over the years, your family has given you every opportunity. You have repeatedly embarrassed them and taken advantage of their kindness. I have watched you torture them over the years with your antics and there is no way that this church would fund you going anywhere near them now. The truth, and I say it with love, is this… You are broken, but obviously not broken enough to understand it. Get out of this church, and leave your father alone… He has forgiven you already and he wants to die in peace."

Mike left the church absolutely stinging at what had just happened. Had Pastor Thomas just thrown him out of the church? Mike stood in the parking lot stunned; this couldn't be the end of it. This was his chance to prove to everyone that he could do something without outside help. He just had to earn some money and get to Germany and make his father proud. Isn't that what this is all about? The only thing standing in his way was a complete lack of funds, but he would work something out.

It had been awhile since he had even looked for a job. Between his mom's generosity, government aid and occasional handyman work, he had managed to get by so far. Mike's philosophy was to suck someone dry for everything he could, then move to take advantage of something else. Not anymore! He was going to prove to the pastor and everyone else that this trip was not about him; he was going to show his father he was not a failure and a leech – he could make it on his own without anyone's handouts.

In a few short days, his enthusiasm dissipated. He felt hopeless; job after job interview ended with the same results. "I'm sorry, you aren't qualified" was always the answer. He knew that his criminal record prevented him from getting the jobs. It didn't matter how well the interview went. The only hope remained a tough construction job that paid pretty well, and the foreman even agreed to give him time to go and see his father when it came to that. What amazed Mike was that he got the job despite being brutally honest with the foreman about his situation; maybe Dad was right all along. If he saved most of his salary for a month he would have enough to buy a ticket to Germany and still have a little bit of spending money. In his mind the plan was solid, he could and he would make things right.

***

John's story spun into a spectacle. The news cameras were everywhere; the discovery of the executed Germans was front page news. John's hospital bed was the target for most of Germany's main networks. The reporters surrounded not only the room, but the hospital. It was one massive media frenzy and even though John couldn't fully understand the news coverage, it seemed they were making him out to be some kind of hero. The initial focus was on the horrors of war, not that he was party to a war crime. Somehow, this story was fueling a discussion on the sacrifice of the German nation during those dark times. He was an ordinary man, put in extraordinary circumstances, who stood by and did nothing in the face of pure evil. He was being treated as a victim of circumstance, not a coward. He understood the empathy but what he wanted was to be cleansed of his sins.

The fact that Brant, a career soldier continuing his family's tradition of service, was on his way to his third tour in Iraq, was also big news. John's war record was plastered on every channel. His life was "the big story." He could feel his gut twist, and he silently prayed for death. How could this be? After all these years, he finally had a chance to make things right, and now he was the hero? It was ludicrous. He started seeing interviews granted to reporters by his battle buddies from Korea and from Vietnam. They were deifying him and he could do nothing about it. He wondered if he could jump out the window or make it back to the house to get one of Brant's weapons. He couldn't stand it anymore. And to top everything, Haas's family was protecting and supporting him. Why did they not hate him as he felt he deserved?

Tanja entered with a news reporter who had managed to break past the lines containing the others and asked, "Papa...will you talk to him?"

John knew that this was his chance. In great detail, he described the final minutes of the Germans, and how he had failed to stop the slaughter. He was in tears and his whole body was convulsing. The only thing he never mentioned was the Journal. He felt that it belonged now to Tanja and to her mother.

The reporter asked all the hard questions, "Do you feel Haas deserved to die?... Do you think that all the Germans were Nazis?... Do you believe in double standards?..."

The inquiries were relentless and after a point, all he could do was to shake his head or nod when appropriate.

He thought with this final confession, it would be

done, but the media intensity only increased. Soon, the backlash hit. News stories talked of the failure of Americans to protect the German populace, the bombings of Dresden. The tone of the reports recalled the darker days and the feelings of WWII. The phone rang incessantly with reporters and the most improbable, people offering book and movie deals. He never thought that he could actually worsen his predicament.

Before this media circus, John lived alone in his private little hell; now his story dragged with him everyone he cared about. Even little Sophia was caught up in all the drama, and was becoming upset every time someone approached her Poppy. Tanja kept quiet but John sensed she was holding something from him. Luckily, the frequency of the reports started to decrease and in less than a week it was over. A crisis had erupted in the Middle East and John Dougall's news cycle ran out and stopped abruptly. No one was talking about him anymore. It was a done deal and time for the funeral of Haas.

CARLA

"O conscience, upright and stainless, how bitter a sting to thee is a little fault!"

DANTE ALIGHERI

They all were back at the house in Bamberg.

Sophia and her grandfather had become instant buddies and inseparable. The connection was a joy to watch. Brant could see how happy John was when he was around her. The old man would tell her stories about when he was a child, when he joined the Army and little Sophia's favorites, about when Brant was her age. Brant could not remember his father being so relaxed since …well, ever.

"Dad, how are you doing?"

"Fine, Son… I'm still processing it all. How are you doing? Are you ready for this next deployment?"

"I'm ready. Just didn't think it would be here so soon. What are your plans now?"

"Brant, to tell you the truth, I thought I would just come here, dig up Haas and then keel over."

Brant recognized his father's famous smirk and felt comforted that his dad had regained some of himself.

"Well, you came close but the doctor says that you're relatively healthy, just overstressed. Dad, I'll be leaving in a few weeks. Do you want to stay on here with Tanja and Sophia?"

"Is Tanja alright with that?"

"We've already discussed it, and you are welcome to stay if you want. I know it would mean a lot to Tanja, and Sophia has really gotten attached to you."

The paradox didn't go unnoticed by either of them; the fact that Tanja grew up without a Grandfather, due in large part to the actions of John. Now, he was in a position to be there for Sophia.

***

"Papa? I don't know if you are up for it but do you want to go with me to see my grandmother Carla? She still lives here, in the old house down by the river."

"Oh dear God!" John panicked. "This is what I hoped for, to ask for forgiveness from her. But…"

"I didn't want to add any more to your stress," Tanja offered with a soothing voice. "I wasn't sure if she would see you, so I just let you assume she was no longer alive. I went to speak with her, and she wants to meet you before the funeral. She is ninety now but she is sharp as a tack. She doesn't miss a thing."

"Tanja, have you talked to her about …"

"Papa, have you been watching the news lately? Your story's been on every channel… She knows everything by now."

As they arrived at Haas's old house, John Sr. could feel sweat bead up on his forehead. He turned and saw Sophia and her beautiful smile.

"You get to meet Oma Carla, Opa!"

"Yes, sweetie, I am very excited." John thought that "terrified" would be more accurate but he put forward a brave smile for the little girl.

In a few minutes, they were at Carla's bedroom door, and Tanja was gently pushing it open. Carla motioned them in, and with that, Sophia ran and jumped into the bed with her Oma. Amid hugs and giggles, Sophia introduced John to Carla.

"Oma, this is my Opa from America."

John could not speak. He was staring at the black and white photo. It was grainy and his vision weak, but he knew… He knew he was looking at Haas and Haas was looking right back. He could almost hear Haas's last words…

"Mr. Dougall, thank you for coming to see me; if you give me a few more minutes with Sophia and Tanja, we can talk. I know we are both a little anxious."

John was taken aback by her perfect English and tone.

Her voice was as a teacher would speak to a student, and he understood that he was about to learn more than he wanted to know. He dutifully went to wait outside.

Tanja and Sophia came out of the room, and Sophia ran up to John and gave him a huge hug.

"Have fun with Oma Carla, Opa! I think she likes you."

"We will wait for you out here, Papa," said Tanja. "Oma tires very easily, so if she tells you what you need; take it as a cue to just say your goodbyes."

Tanja had chosen the name Sophia and said that its meaning of wisdom was in honor of Oma Carla. A chill came over him as he remembered the conversation. Tanja had prepared him as best she could.

John entered the room and pulled up a chair to where Carla had motioned him to be, near her. He found her so graceful and well put together, not what you would expect for someone even older than him.

"John, thank you for coming to see me. I know that you have been through a lot and that you want to tell me your story. So tell me…"

John felt overwhelmed. Here he was sitting inches from his Carla Haas, but couldn't form the words to tell her what he had wanted to say for so long. His mind raced back –one more time– to that accursed April morning. He could see the condemned Germans. Why didn't he step in? Why did he let the Sergeant execute them? His stomach turned and twisted with each detail remembered. He saw his squad mates digging through the pockets of the dead… stripping them of watches, wallets and uniform badges. He knew he had to do the same so that McGee wouldn't shoot him. The Sergeant had already said as much when John started to intervene and to try to preserve the dignity of the dead.

He remembered putting his hand inside the thick wool

jacket, the firm texture of the Journal and its rough, leather binding. He removed it and held it up to the Sergeant. As he turned back to the German, he stared right into the eyes of a dying man. The German whispered, "*Wasser, ich moechte Wasser.*" It was then he saw the light leave his eyes.

The weight of the Journal increased day by day, and over the years he had only been able to open it up for a few brief moments at a time. He saw the picture of the beautiful brunette, the postcards from France... and the name on the inner cover - Haas. The information he did glean from the Journal caused John to reflect, every day, on the possibility that his action or inaction severed the blood-line of a noble enemy. John Sr. did not want to die knowing that he was not strong enough to do the right thing. He had been given life by the enemy, the day the tanker had chosen not to fire. War is chaos, yet every decision causes a chain of events often only known to God. Why was he spared? And when he was given the chance to save a life, he faltered. Now it was time to confess – how he failed.

John let it all out in great detail. He spoke of the executions and the years after in which he kept the Journal and how he was haunted by what he did not prevent. Carla did not show any emotion. She simply sat there and nodded when appropriate and let him talk.

"John, do you feel any different now? Did it bring you the closure you were looking for? Or do you need my forgiveness? If that is what you are seeking, I want you to know that you have had it for many years.

You see John, after the war, I spent every waking moment looking for Rudi. In the late 1950s, I discovered a direct connection between your unit and the last, known location of my husband. McGee had written a letter to his family confessing what he did; it was less of a confession than a bold assertion of what he considered a just killing over the loss of his brother at Malmedy. Oddly, he

mentioned you by name, Private Dougall. He said specifi-
cally that he almost had to put a hole in your head because
you tried to protect the Nazis."

John again felt overwhelmed. He cleared his throat
and asked, "Mrs. Haas, how did you find such a letter?"

"After the war, there was a huge push by all parties of
the war to recover their dead. When a German would find
an American, we would turn them over to the American
Mortuary Affairs and the same happened when Germans
were found by Americans. On our side we did one additional thing. The Germans copied all the papers found with
the American dead. McGee happened to be one of those
Americans. A late friend of mine, Hans Beck – you probably know the name from the Journal -found the letter for
me in some archive. Another friend helped me track down
an American soldier named John Dougall, stationed in
Bamberg, ten years after the war. That is right John, just as
you have held on to that Journal and couldn't bring it back
to me, I couldn't forgive you and let you know that you
were not to blame. I am sorry for that.

The other thing you must know is that my friend at
that time was a very beautiful young British student. I
asked her to meet you so that through her, I could be closer
to you and perhaps find out more details. What I hadn't
counted on was that she would fall in love."

John's heart started pounding so hard that he thought
it would jump out of his chest. He flashed back to the night
at the dance hall when the attractive blonde smiled at him.
My Margarie… Carla's spy?

John caught himself smiling nostalgically, in awe that
his better half had kept this lifelong secret from him.

"Well… she gave me her heart and made my life bear-
able." He could feel a divine hand in all of this. He leaned

closer to Carla, and looking into her eyes, slowly handed her the Journal.

Carla clasped the Journal to her breast and inhaled sharply.

"John, you said you failed because you didn't risk your life for what was right. I can't forgive you, because you have done nothing wrong. That man murdered Rudi, not you! Please forgive yourself and look at what your decision has created. You lived... and that led to the joy of holding my dear Sophia. Soon Tanja will have another child. We must finish what you have come here for so we can focus on the living."

As John left, he thought:

The Dougall clan has earned a noble German graft onto the family tree. The idea brought him peace at last; and self-forgiveness.

***

Mike sat back on his couch clutching almost two grand in cash. It was an honest wage from the past month's work. He was tired and euphoric. He struck a good deal with a travel agency, which would leave him almost a thousand bucks to spend on a rental car and hotel room. He wouldn't need to ask anyone for anything. He could just pop in for a visit and show them all he was his own man.

As he looked at the money sitting in his hand, Mike thought that he might just get a little taste to knock off the edge. It had been awhile since he used. Brimming with self-confidence, Mike felt in control. He had a long flight ahead of him, and he longed for some much needed rest. All he wanted was just one fix to help calm him down. His buddy would hook him up with a nice cocktail, and he could even throw in a couple of pills for the plane ride.

The drug dealer came over to the apartment, excited to see one of his best customers with some cash to spend. In a matter of hours, Mike lay on the floor in a pool of his own vomit; penniless, drugged to near death, dreaming of the perfect reunion with his father… one that would never come.

EPILOGUE

Rudolf Haas was buried properly on a cold, Saturday morning. A German-American squad jointly presented him with military honors. Even little Sophia was quiet, intimidated by the solemnity of the ceremony. Only two lines appeared on the simple, stone cross:

RUDOLF HAAS

16.7.1920 – 13.4.1945

GLOSSARY

Places:

Anapa: small Black Sea city-port in Russia, near the Azov Sea. Germany occupied and held Anapa until September 1943.

Ardennes: forested hilly region in Belgium. The Germans crossed it and surprised the French in 1940. They attempted another surprise attack in the winter of 1944 that resulted in the Battle of the Bulge.

Argentan: town in north-western France. The Battle of the Falaise Pocket was fought near Argentan in August 1944.

Baku: important city port at the Caspian Sea. Today is the capital of Azerbaijan.

Bamberg: city in Bavaria, Germany. Its unique medieval appearance survived the horrors of WWII bombings.

Caucasus: region between the Black Sea and the Caspian Sea. It separates European Russia from Southeast Asia. It includes the Caucasus Mountains, the highest in Europe.

Crimea: peninsula in Southern Russia. It withstood numerous invasions in history. During WWII, it was occupied by Germany and Romania until 1944.

Don: river in Russia. Between Don's bend and Volga the Soviets launched Operation Uranus (November 1942) - the highly successful counterattack that trapped the Germans at Stalingrad.

Elbrus: Caucasus Mountains' tallest peak at 5,642 meters (18,510 ft). During the 1942 German offensive, a group of Gebirgsjäger (mountain troops) planted the swastika flag at its top.

Hermannnstadt: city in southern Transylvania (Romania). It was founded by German settlers in 12th century. The Romanian name is Sibiu. In Hungarian is called Nagyszeben.

Kuban: region in southern Russia. The Germans held a bridgehead in Kuban until October 1943.

Kursk: site of the last Wehrmacht attempt to knock out the Red Army. The battle resulted in a tactical stalemate and a major strategic defeat for Nazi Germany.

Livadia Palace: summer residence of the Russian tsars. It came under German control when von Manstein conquered Crimea. In 1945, Livadia Palace hosted the Yalta Conference (the far reaching meeting between Stalin Roosevelt and Churchill)

Meuse: river flowing through France, Belgium and Netherland

Nalchik: city in southern Russia, founded in the early 19th century when the Russian Empire started to expand into the Caucasus. During WWII it was briefly occupied by Germany and Romania.

Odessa: city in Ukraine. During WWII Odessa was occupied by Romanian Army.

Prokhorovka: site of the largest tank battle in WWII. Hundreds of German tanks clashed with a higher number of Soviet tanks. It was a draw.

Rathaus: city hall (German)

Remagen: German city on the Rhine. In March 1945, the bridge at Remagen was captured by US 9th Armored Division.

Rostov-on-Don: city in Russia, just north of the Black Sea. Its strategic position made Rostov-on-Don a battleground contested by Germany and U.S.S.R. in 1941, 1942 and 1943.

Siebenburger: Transylvania (German); named after the seven major Saxon cities founded by the German colonists in Transylvania.

Siegburg: German city north of Remagen

Schlenkerla: famous pub in Bamberg, known for their "smoked" dark beer

Simferopol: city in Crimea

Stalingrad: city on Volga (today's Volgograd). Between August 1942 and February 1943, Stalingrad witnessed the most brutal battle of WWII. The decisive Soviet victory marked the turning point in the war.

Volga: river in Russia, largest in Europe. The Germans reached it at Stalingrad.

Weyermann Malt Factory: Specialty malts factory in Bamberg, Germany.

Military vocabulary, ranks and equipment:

37mm anti-tank gun (PanzerabwehrKanone aka Pak 36): small caliber anti-tank gun. Pak 36 proved ineffectual against most Soviet tanks.

88mm anti-tank gun: best German anti-tank weapon in WWII. It was designed originally as an anti-aircraft gun. Erwin Rommel employed it very successfully in North Africa against the British.

Flak (Flugzeugabwehr-Kanone): anti-aircraft artillery (German)

Hawker-Typhoon: long range British fighter-bomber

Hauptmann: Captain (German)

Heinkel He 111: versatile German bomber used throughout WWII

KV-1 (Kliment Voroshilov): Soviet heavy tank. Its thick armor made this machine almost impervious to most anti-tank fire. The Soviets developed more models based on this design, the most impressive being IS-1 (Iosif Stalin).

Leutnant: Lieutenant (German)

Luftwaffe: German Air Force.

MACV (Military Assistance Command Vietnam): U.S. command structure for all of its military forces in South Vietnam. Located in Saigon, it was disbanded in 1973. *NCO*: non-commissioned officer

Oberkommando der Wehrmacht (OKW): Germany's Military General Staff during WWII. Hitler's tight control decreased OKW's effectiveness.

Oberstleutnant: Lieutenant Colonel (German)

P38 Lightning: American-made, long-range fighter aircraft employed in Europe, Africa and Pacific in WWII

Panzer IV: most ubiquitous of all German tanks. A reliable design, it featured a three man turret (commander, gunner and loader) a driver and a radio operator. The initial models had relatively thin armor and a short ineffectual gun. In 1942, the introduction of a long-barreled 75mm gun and armor upgrades made Panzer IV capable of successfully engaging the Russian KV-1 and T-34 tanks.

Panzerkampfwagen V (Panther): best medium German tank of WWII. The Germans were never able to field them in sufficient numbers to turn the tide of the war.

POW: prisoner of war

Panzerkampfwagen VI (Tiger): German heavy tank. The Tiger models equipped with the 88mm gun could knock any other tank from a safe distance. It was introduced too late in the war to make a difference.

R and R, R&R (rest and relaxation): US military abbreviation for a mid-tour leave during a deployment

Romanian Mountain Troops: specialized infantry- widely regarded as the best trained and equipped in the Romanian Army.

Sherman: the main American tank in WWII. U.S. produced massive numbers of Sherman tanks and provided a number of them to the Soviets, British and French forces.

T-34: most effective Soviet tank design in WWII. It combined firepower, mobility, protection and reliability. Cheap and built in huge numbers, the T-34 could be regarded as the weapon that won WWII. Although obsolete by 1950, upgraded T-34s proved deadly in the early stages of the Korean War.

Unteroffizier: NCO/Sergeant

Wehrmacht: German Armed Forces

Foreign words/expressions/organizations:

Adler: eagle (German)

Babushka: grandmother (Russian)

Bahnhof: train station (German)

Auf den Boden: hit the ground (German)

Da, domnule capitan: Yes, Sir/ Captain (Romanian)

Hitlerjugend: Hitler Youth

Hoch: up (German)

Junkers: Prussian nobles traditionally involved in the Prussian/German military

Rasputitsa: Russia's season of bad roads. The muddy unpaved roads made any troop and supplies movement extremely difficult during the fall and spring.

NKVD (Narodnyy Komissariat Vnutrennikh Del): The People Commissariat for Internal Affairs – Soviet secret police, later changed its name to KGB.

SD (Sicherheitsdienst): the intelligence service of SS

SMS Emden: famous German warship in WWI. Emden sunk thirty Allied vessels before was destroyed by HMAS Sydney - an Australian cruiser.

Volkssturm: German militia in WWII

Waffen-SS: a multinational military force of the Nazi Party. It became an elite military force but many SS units were involved in odious war crimes against civilians (Holocaust) and against POWs.

Wasser, ich moechte Wasser: Water, I would like water.

German Military Awards:

German Cross in Gold: German award for bravery during WWII

Knight's Cross of Iron Cross: highest German award for bravery during WWII

Editor's Notes:

Dear Reader,

You may find yourself or aspects of your life's experiences in this story presented for you by first time authors Captains Brookshire and Tecoanta. Perhaps you've encountered similar characters in life, in books or in films. The people on these pages are fused from the writers' real life experiences and those of their battle buddies, their families, interview subjects and of course, historical data. The book's segments are written alternately to reflect the two author's voices as well as the times in which truths about lives and relationships are revealed.

You and I are invited to witness the fallout from being on the frontlines of trauma, loss, regret and war times that rob, but we also look in on love and hope. The particular people we get to know negotiate the impact of wounds inflicted physically and emotionally in faraway places, but dealt with at home. Somewhere from within the hearts of the soldiers and their families, you may experience insights about your own daily life's challenges and solutions.

My role as editor was to smooth the way for you to travel into the story. I hoped most to preserve the voice and spirit of the authors as they expressed, from a soldier's point of view, the era's personalities, issues and emotions.

If you ask them, Nathan Brookshire and Marius Tecoanta will tell you that in the writing, "Things came out that were not expected." I hope you enjoy the layers of life they've written about with such passion and dedication. You may discover that the story has deepened your self-knowledge and entices you into ongoing discussions within your community, as you define it. To this I can only add, "Write on!"

— Helena Kaufman

Hidden Wounds

A 501(c)(3) Non-Profit Organization

Hidden Wounds seeks to educate the community on the severe effects that psychological stress injuries are causing. One in four of our military veterans suffer from these injuries daily and fight to overcome them on our very own American soil. Hidden Wounds provides private counseling services to any military veteran or active-duty military personnel suffering from Post-Traumatic Stress Disorder (PTSD), Traumatic Brain Injury (TBI) and/or depression. Hidden Wounds aims to lower the rising rate of suicide among our military veterans by helping heroes battle the invisible war at home.

"I feel like everyone can see what I've done. I can't live this way."

-M P Bigham

Brief History of the Organization

Hidden Wounds was formed in response to a tragedy involving its founder, Anna Bigham. Anna's brother, Lance Corporal Mills Palmer Bigham, served four years of active duty for the United States Marine Corps. LCpl Bigham served two tours of duty in Iraq with Weapons Company, 1st Battalion, 2nd Regiment. He was released from active duty on October 19, 2008, with an honorable discharge and new rank, Combat Veteran. Immediately, Anna recognized her brother was not the same young man she once knew. LCpl Bigham sought treatment for war trauma, 180 depression, and anger through numerous trips to the local VA hospital. He was diagnosed with Post Traumatic Stress Disorder (PTSD), however, he was not given the treatment he deserved. Anna made countless phone calls to check on his status for receiving those services, but each time there was very little to no response. Anna supported her brother, battled for his right to treatment, and cared for him during the long and horrific nights. It was too little, and too late. Mills took his own life, waiting for those services, on October 19, 2009.

Shortly thereafter, Anna decided that she could not let her brother's death be the way out for any more of our heroes. It is her dedication and passion to prevent her tragic story from happening to others that has brought us here today.

Hidden Wounds was founded in memory of Marine, Lance Corporal Mills Palmer Bigham. 04/08/1986 - 10/19/2009.

Contact Info:

Hidden Wounds Inc.
501c3 non-profit organization
Helping Heroes Battle The Invisible War At Home

Hidden Wounds
7001 St Andrews Road #323
Columbia, SC 29212
1-888-4HW-HERO
803.403.8460 main
866.764.4030 fax
Hiddenwounds.org
info@hiddenwounds.org
Anna Bigham, Founder Annab@hiddenwounds.org

Organizations Partnered with HiddenWounds.org

Give an Hour™
Give help | Give hope

Give an Hour is a nonprofit 501(c)(3), founded in September 2005 by Dr. Barbara Van Dahlen, a psychologist in the Washington, D.C., area. The organization's mission is to develop national networks of volunteers capable of responding to both acute and chronic conditions that arise within our society. Currently, GAH is dedicated to meeting the mental health needs of the troops and families affected by the ongoing conflicts in Iraq and Afghanistan. Give an Hour has providers across the nation—in all 50 states, the District of Columbia, and Puerto Rico—and continues to recruit volunteer mental health professionals to its network. Mental health professionals interested in joining Give an Hour can complete an easy on-line form at www.giveanhour.org.

Mission: TAPS provides ongoing emotional help, hope, and healing to all who are grieving the death of a loved one in military service to America, regardless of relationship to the deceased, geography, or circumstance of the death. TAPS meets its mission by providing peer-based support, crisis care, casualty casework assistance, and grief and trauma resources.

If you are suffering the loss of a military loved one, or if you know someone who can use our support, please call our toll-free hotline now: 1-800-959-TAPS (8277). www.taps.org

Bonnie Carroll, Founder & President
Info@taps.org

MISSION: Operation Homefront (OH) provides emergency financial and other assistance to the families of our service members and wounded warriors.

VISION: Through generous, widespread public support and a collaborative team of exceptional staff and volunteers, we aspire to become the provider of choice for emergency financial and other assistance to the families of our service members and wounded warriors. Where there is a need we do not provide, we will partner with others for the benefit of our military families.

Sharon Rice
President

Operation Homefront of South Carolina
PO Box 6883
Columbia, SC 29260
O: 866-457-2093   C: 803-465-3284

Nathan Brookshire is currently serving as an active duty commissioned officer with the United States Army. "Nate" has enjoyed a successful 20-year career with multiple deployments in combat zones. He lives in Columbia, South Carolina with his wife and children.

Marius Tecoanta is a commissioned officer with the Oregon National Guard. "T" has had a diverse career in manufacturing, law enforcement and military. He lives in Beaverton, Oregon with his wife and son.